DAISIES DON'T tell

Daisies Don't tell

Lorayne Orton Smith

Rutledge Books, Inc.   Danbury, CT

Interior design by Elena Hartz

Copyright © 2002 by Lorayne Orton Smith

ALL RIGHTS RESERVED
Rutledge Books, Inc.
107 Mill Plain Road, Danbury, CT 06811
1-800-278-8533
www.rutledgebooks.com

Manufactured in the United States of America

Cataloging in Publication Data
Smith, O. Lorayne
    Daisies Don't Tell

    ISBN: 1-58244-205-3

    1. Fiction.

Library of Congress Control Number: 2002100355

To my family and families everywhere.

* * * * *

A special acknowledgement to my husband, Vernon, for his enduring support and to Katherine B. Watson for her computer skills in typing my manuscript and her longtime encouragement in my writing this story.

1

The clock ticked slowly toward the happy hour of four in the old red brick Mechanic Arts High School in St. Paul. Outside, the early March thaw, hinting that spring was near, competed with the discussion in Miss Daisy Coolidge's English class. Her classes were always interesting for she was not yet locked into the rigid mold of many old maid schoolteachers.

Her merry dark eyes, high intelligent forehead and tall, well-proportioned figure all denoted an alert, capable young woman. In her mid-thirties, she exuded the confidence and poise gained from holding a responsible position in the work of one's choice.

But this afternoon, even her interest in the Romantic poets lagged and it was a relief when she noticed the clock nearing four. Suddenly the hum of activity over the room stilled as a smartly uniformed Western Union boy strode in. He handed an envelope to the teacher, and marched out, trying hard to appear unaware of the thirty pairs of eyes following him.

Telegrams-those yellow messages that always presage calamity to their recipients. It is true that good news also can be sent by wire, but to most people, a telegram quickens the heart and catches the breath in anxious anticipation.

🌼 Daisies Don't Tell

Miss Coolidge had opened the yellow envelope and was standing where she had received it, scanning the few lines. Outside, the twitter of chickadees was the only sound heard in the room.

"School is dismissed," the teacher announced abruptly. Half-quieted by her serious face, yet glad of a few extra minutes of freedom, the seniors hurried off, forgetting as they entered the student congestion in the hall, the unnatural silence they had just left.

Alone in her room, Miss Coolidge gazed out over Wabasha Avenue, the disgraceful approach to the beautiful capitol of a proud state. Her sister, Myrtice, whom she loved more than any other person on earth, was ill. To receive word of a sister's illness anytime is disconcerting, but in 1919, illness usually meant one thing—the dreaded influenza. It, like the Black Plague centuries earlier in Europe, left only grief and despair in its trail.

Myrtice, her smiling, happy sister, whose five pregnancies in seven years had seemingly never dampened her spirits, sick. It seemed impossible. But the practical nature in Miss Coolidge, probably inherited from Scottish/Dutch ancestors, soon caused her to abandon sad musing and make plans.

She needed to go at once to be with her sister. Herbert, her brother-in-law, had clearly intimated that in his few conventional phrases. Those few stark words only vaguely resembled the genial hard-working man to whom her sister had been so happily married for the past decade.

Securing a substitute, preparing lesson outlines, explaining in writing to her totally deaf mother who lived with her, obtaining train schedules, took the rest of her day.

Flora Jane Coolidge, a sweet-faced, large woman confined to a wheelchair, was cheerful when she read the news (the seriousness of which Daisy had minimized) written in her youngest daughter's beautiful Palmer-method-trained handwriting.

"Tell Herb hello," were her parting words as her daughter left early next morning. At the depot, Daisy sensed that her personal troubles were only part of a heavy blanket of sorrow spread over the nation with the aftermath of World War I and the accompanying flu epidemic. On the three-hour train ride through the wooded, rolling countryside of central Minnesota, Daisy had leisure to think for the first time since she had received the upsetting telegram.

Her sister's life was so closely intertwined with hers. As children, they had been inseparable playmates, the two years between them only strengthening the bond as they grew older.

Myrtie, Daisy thought fondly, using the family pet name, had taught school a year after graduating from high school so they could both enter college together. At Graylin University, a sedate Methodist school, the oldest in the state, Myrtie had been popular with the boys, just as she had been in their rural home community.

There was never any question whether Myrtie would go to the ice cream socials as she always had male companions. Boys hanging around, trying to flirt with clumsy words of flattery one knew they didn't mean-Daisy still felt her old disgust for men in general.

Myrtice, she reflected, was pretty and sweet. She could laugh merrily, no matter how stupid her escort might act. But for Daisy, who was well aware she lacked her sister's appeal, the bubbling small talk never came without effort. Because she always had excelled in scholarship, Daisy had decided early in life to concentrate on her studies, developing a nonchalant exterior toward social life. Already she had taught in several towns; had even served as superintendent in the small town of Goose Lake. Indeed, she was one of the first women in the state to hold such a position, and she had met and worked with many men. One school board member had been determined to propose, despite her attempts to deflect his interest.

But looking out on the Mississippi River, rough with broken ice, Daisy thought with a sigh of the old maxim that a girl with a college degree seldom has the fun her less educated sisters do. A man must be intelligent, gentlemanly, yet know his way around, like Herb, she mused, as the train sped by the hamlet of Elk Grove, across the river from where both the Coolidges and the Nortons, Herb's family, had grown up.

Suddenly, the icy realization that Myrtie was deathly sick, possibly dead by now, caused her to start guiltily at her own thoughts. Her duty now was to help with the housework in the Norton home, tend her sister's five children-from baby Juanita, seventeen months old, to Floyd, eight, a dark-eyed lad who was her favorite nephew.

After that?-she wondered with an odd feeling in her throat. But like a warm wave covering the beach, a hope strong enough to seem true, swept over her-of course Myrtie would live, she simply couldn't die with a brood of children and a husband who needed her.

This faith sustained her when, at the depot in Croquille, she saw Herb's stricken face, which looked older than his thirty-five years, and witnessed the domestic turmoil in the roomy, white farmhouse three miles north of town where her sister and husband had moved only the previous year.

With quiet manner, Daisy soon made her presence appreciated. Grace, the hired girl who also was serving as nurse, was hopelessly incapable of making the children mind, as well as too busy in the sickroom to have time to adequately look after them. It was a relief to Daisy to be able to tire herself with physical labor. Since the sick woman was unconscious and attended by the doctor and practical nurse, the schoolteacher took over the housework.

Washing dishes on a farm, especially breakfast dishes, is different from coping with the few utensils used in a city kitchen which are washed in a neat little sink in a few minutes. On a farm-a dairy farm at least-the china is only the first course. There are milk containers, large eighteen-quart pails to which milk clots and froth like to cling, and eight-gallon cans which hold the milk.

These have to be lifted into the long sink, scrubbed, and rinsed. Then there was the separator which divided the whole milk into cream and skim milk-ever a source of wonder to non-farm children-with its disks and spouts, all needing to be carefully washed and rinsed.

Is it any mystery that farm women should complain of aching backs? Electricity now has removed much of the drudgery in farm life, but labor-saving devices were then unknown and electricity confined to cities.

As the days passed, Daisy's long, slim fingers became roughened from continual washing and scrubbing. But housework was nothing new to her, having grown up in a poor home where everyone had learned to work.

It soon became apparent that Myrtice, only mechanically alive in a coma, might remain in that state for weeks. It seemed less likely each day that she would ever regain consciousness. These words, driving like hail on the hard pavement, raced through Daisy's brain. She wrote and obtained a month's leave of absence from her school. One afternoon, after she had straightened the house and sent the smaller children outside to play, she sat mending in the dining room, always referred to as the sitting room.

Through the window, the blue of the Father of Waters could be seen across a newly plowed field and a pasture showing the first green grass. Herb's step startled her. What could bring her brother-in-law in from his seeding in the middle of the afternoon, she wondered, as her steady hand deftly mended a torn shirt.

Herb, hesitating in the short hallway between the kitchen and dining room, paused, vaguely realizing that a semblance of order had returned to his house since his sister-in-law had come. Whether it was the clean curtains or the early spring violets artistically arranged on the oak dining room table, he didn't know, but those Coolidge girls certainly had a way with their hands, he mused.

"Daisy," he broke the strained hesitation between them abruptly, "you know she can't live." The words seemed torn from him. A swift surge of pity for this man overcame her personal sense of loss. She looked into his gray-blue eyes, startled by their intensity, and realized he was faced with the overwhelming task of raising five small children without his wife.

"But she may regain consciousness." Her words, in an effort to comfort, were low and urgent. "Don't give up hoping and praying, Herb."

The young farmer sank wearily into a chair, his drooping shoulders showing more clearly than words his utter despair.

"I know." Common experiences in church and Epworth League in their youth now stabilized the bond between them.

"God can't take her! It's not for myself, but the children. Judas Priest," his favorite expression, "what can I do?" His agonized words brought tears to Daisy's eyes. Why was life so unfair? Devious, crafty men she knew seemed blessed by Lady Luck, while someone like Herb. . .

She spoke gently, with the faith gained from years of companionship with and study of Christianity giving confidence to her voice: "It's not always for us to know God's will, or to understand His wishes, Herb. Our duty is to bear what comes bravely." The last words sank to a whisper. Who was she to talk so glibly of bravery to this man who stood before her straight and strong, his eyes steady and clear? He was obviously facing the biggest crisis of his life.

Somehow their talk had given confidence to them both. Tramping back to the field where the resting team was contentedly chewing tender young brush, Herb wondered how long his sister-in-law would stay. It was a blessing she was here, he mused, with the children getting out of hand. School would be out soon, maybe she'd be kind enough to stay through till fall.

She'd always been kind, he reflected. Myrtie's little sister had been part of the young people's group at the little white country church where he had fallen in love with Myrtice. He dimly remembered that when his parents had moved to the community when he was a teenager, he first had shown interest in Daisy, who was a little younger than he, while Myrtice was a year older.

What he was unaware of was the gentle manipulation of his mother in directing his attention to the older girl, mostly because she was more outgoing. Herb held his mother in high regard and would have been surprised had anyone told him that he had been maneuvered. Lavonia Norton had been a workaholic, typical of her New England ancestry. Married to a mate with a much less serious attitude toward life, she perhaps felt this serious son, with many of her characteristics, needed someone with a lighter touch. Happily married and working long hours as a farmer, he never had given a second thought to his choice of the Coolidge sisters.

Back in the farmhouse, Daisy struggled with conflicting thoughts. Her month's leave of absence was nearly gone; the principal had written urging her to resume her work, citing as arguments for her return, the inadequacies of her substitute and the lowering of disciplinary standards among what had been the best senior section.

The last phrase had made Daisy contemptuous; if she were back in the classroom there would be no lowering of disciplinary standards! Even the phrase annoyed her. The substitute couldn't make the students mind, that was obvious. Yet it would be cruel to leave her nieces and nephews to the hit-and-miss care of hired help. Surely she was needed here.

Would Myrtie's condition ever change? This thought chased all others out of consideration in her mind. Frantically she prayed that her sister might live, that the crisis would come soon. The tension was maddening. That night as the family ate at the supper table, lighted by the flickering kerosene lamp, a remark from Jean, the second girl and middle child, pierced whatever hope Daisy still had for her sister's recovery.

"When will Mama die?" the youngster piped in her childish voice, merely parroting words dropped carelessly by the hired girl/nurse. The silence following her innocent query was broken by her father on a safer subject.

"Sit up and eat your carrots, Neil," Herb tersely ordered his younger son who, with all the determination of his nearly four years had thrust the offending carrots, golden with butter, to one side of his plate. Worry exacts a cruel toll, thought Daisy, as she observed the gruff, sharp manner her brother-in-law took with his children. Indeed, they were beginning to avoid him, when in happier days they had run to him with delight.

Children should always be treated with firmness tempered with kindness, she knew, but if she remained, the work and worry would, no doubt, make her as ungentle as well. The poor children, she mused, their lot was to either be kept together by a father too worn by worry to think of their emotional needs or else be divided among the many brothers and sisters of their parents.

They shan't be separated-the grim determination on her face melted into a smile at Carol, the eldest daughter, age seven, who with her big brown eyes and thin face looked pensive. A perceptive child, mature for her age as befits the oldest daughter, she was more aware of what was happening than any of her siblings.

The dreaded question of the whole family was soon answered. One evening the sick woman stirred, muttering deliriously. The fever had broken, helped by heated corncobs brought from the kitchen cookstove oven to her bed by her devoted caretakers. But too much poison to be overcome had filled the weakened body; antibiotics were yet unknown. That evening the young mother died, without regaining consciousness. Wrenching as deathbed scenes are, they nevertheless provide an emotional finality for those left behind.

Herb, crushed in sorrow, had been denied even a farewell. If only, he raged inwardly, he could have told her at the last how much he loved her, how greatly he would miss her, what a wonderful partner she had been. Bitterness tinged the numbing sorrow that saturated his mind as he gazed dumbly at his dead wife's face. To bring her flowers now, as seemed expected of him, when he never once had brought her a bouquet during their marriage, except the wildflowers he sometimes picked, seemed to him an empty mockery.

Poor as most young couples starting out in married life, they never had had money to patronize florists. So when he laid down a five-dollar bill on the counter in the floral shop the day before the funeral, the effort to control his self-disgust made his hand shake.

"That fellow's really uptight," muttered the old florist as he watched Herb hurry away.

Daisy moved in a blur through the days before the funeral. She had no time to indulge in personal grief or explain anything to the children. Housework, preparing food for those who would come, and the increasing insistence from well meaning relatives that one child should go here, another two there, kept her in a state of mental confusion. To all suggestions of the children's separation, Daisy merely tightened her lips and spoke clearly of the merits of waiting until everyone got his breath.

She did not know that Eva, her older sister and only living one now, had accosted Herb, giving him a severe tongue-lashing for his refusal to allow her to take Carol and Juanita.

"You wouldn't treat your colts the way you do your children," she stormed, "leaving that baby to the care of hired girls." Eva was large, like her mother, and so crippled with rheumatism that she walked bent over. She was known for her scathing tongue and bad humor.

Herb, who had never liked her since his courting days when she was always demanding that Myrtie, her favorite sister, stay with her over weekends, trembled with indignation at her untactful and cruel remarks. If she weren't a woman and a Coolidge, he'd tell her . . .

Slowly, as if despairing of gaining her understanding, he said, "The children are all I have left now, can't you see, Eva?" His dignity and appeal to her parental instinct only produced a mumbled retort as Eva strode away.

The devil certainly was after him, Herb reflected moodily as he fled to the barn. Although a religious man, reared in the Methodist church, he could not help but believe certain Indian folklore retained by his pioneer ancestors. He recalled that one night just after they had moved to the farm the previous March, a loon had curdled the stillness with its chilling screech. While he had mildly wondered then what ill luck would befall, Herb thought with a start that losing his wife could be only part of the trouble which lay ahead. His mind reeled at the dark future, and to deaden his thoughts, he began cleaning the horse barn furiously.

During the simple service conducted by the Methodist minister in the farmhouse parlor, Daisy decided she would leave that weekend and teach through the remainder of the term. There was nothing to be gained by her staying. She would only make enemies of Herb's six brothers and sisters. After all, what Herb did was none of her business, yet he needed someone . . . her thoughts strayed until the closing prayer.

She accepted his silence as approval when she told him her plans the next day. And with a last Saturday cleaning and the promise of returning in June to her wide-eyed, silent nieces and nephews, Daisy went back to St. Paul.

She had been gone only a month, yet those days of hard physical work on the farm somehow had seemed more satisfying than teaching, much as she enjoyed her profession. The copy of Browning poems she found on her desk with a welcome back card and bouquet made her return to teaching doubly pleasant.

🌼 Daisies Don't Tell

Yet, as she slipped back into the pleasant, intellectual atmosphere of a city schoolteacher, something seemed to be lacking.

One Saturday afternoon when she and a group of teacher friends went to a lecture and dinner, a remark by one of the women began to ferment in Daisy's mind during the half-hour streetcar ride back to her apartment.

"It doesn't matter how successful you are," Miss Blake had said, "a career just doesn't satisfy a woman-she wants to belong." Yes, Daisy mused, a woman needed to belong somewhere.

When school was out in early June, Daisy and her mother closed the five-room flat which had seemed so homelike to them and moved to the farm north of Croquille on June 10, the date of Herb and Myrtice's wedding anniversary.

2

The harvest truly is great, but the laborers are few . . .
— St. Luke 10:2

Daisy soon found that not only had she accepted a job which taxed her physical endurance, but also that she was in a delicate position which called for all her tact. The children, upset and confused about their mother's disappearance, and unruly from three months of no systematic discipline, were ill-disposed to take kindly to their aunt's insistence of immediate obedience. It would be a long summer!

While her heart yearned for them, her educator's mind knew that pity would only produce more self-pity, so with all her energy she planned brisk days of work and play. And always she was willing to talk of their mother who, she told Carol, had merely gone to a distant land where one day they would again see her.

She saw little of Herb for he was outside from dawn until late at night. When the milking was finished, the cows driven to pasture, the milk run through the hand-operated separator and the skim milk, referred to as separator milk, fed to the calves and pigs, Herb and the hired man shuffled wearily to bed. There was neither time nor energy for any of the social amenities common to evenings in the city.

At first, Daisy thought he was deliberately avoiding her, which was natural enough, she thought, since her dark eyes and hair could only remind him of his dead sweetheart. And the outward resemblance would be only more bitter because of the difference in personalities. Daisy swallowed her feeling of offense at his avoidance and used her common sense to analyze his feelings.

But, as the weeks passed and the children (always an accurate gauge in discerning the subtle currents in their elders' actions) showed no surprise at their father merely pulling off his shoes, washing at the kitchen sink, and disappearing into the bedroom which he shared with his sons, Daisy realized this was the usual routine.

She quickly learned, with unpleasant surprise, that evenings with a definite time for relaxation and enjoyment were unknown on this farm. Not that Daisy was the type who wanted to go somewhere every night for neither by inclination nor upbringing did she crave social life. Rather, she always had been disposed to entertain herself by reading, sewing, or playing the piano, on which she was modestly proficient.

But, after being used to the conventional division of the twenty-four hours into morning, afternoon, and evening, she was unaccustomed to having the men sometimes not appear until 1:30 or 2 P.M. for dinner, and anytime in the evening for supper, depending on their occupation.

When she mentioned this to the girls, Carol informed her with childish frankness, "Oh, we never used to eat until Dad got ready to come in. Mama always said she never served a hot meal to a Norton yet." Daisy believed her.

As the weeks went by, she became better acquainted with her two oldest nieces. Carol, a Coolidge by her coloring, although only seven, was capable and dependable, especially in mothering her baby sister, Juanita. It was harder to communicate with blond-haired, green-eyed Jean, who seemed very dependent on her older sister.

Daisy was only vaguely aware of the mental confusion their mother's death had left in the children. At the approaching death they had been packed off to the town home of Linnie Campbell, Herb's oldest sister. They had not been prepared, let alone given any explanation of what had happened.

Upon their return to the farm after the funeral, Jean had wandered around searching for her lost mother. Spotting several empty long white boxes in the basement, she, as always, turned to her older sister to learn what they were. "Those are the boxes which held flowers for Mama's funeral," Carol informed her. Not wanting to appear stupid again, Jean refrained from asking what a funeral was.

In keeping with the ideas of the time, the Campbells had arranged for someone to care for the children during the funeral to shield them from the realities of life, not realizing they were unwittingly adding to the children's trauma. They simply had no idea why their mother had gone out of their lives. Floyd particularly felt abandoned, apparently oblivious to the long weeks his mother was in bed. Carol somehow sensed the reality but the others were too young to long dwell on her disappearance.

While Daisy was well-versed in and could articulate ably the difference between classical and romantic genres of literature, college training prior to her graduation in 1908 did not include even one psychology course and she had no understanding of the children's need to talk about their feelings. She prayed that over time, loving care, kindness, and work would eventually heal their grief.

She had the older two girls do dishes, sweep, and dust, but the bulk of the housework was on her shoulders. She rose at five and cooked breakfast, toasting what seemed like entire loaves of bread over the cookstove for the family. Neil still had to be helped to dress and even though it was Carol's duty, Daisy's supervision was needed. Then there was the toddler to bathe, the milk pails and separator to wash, and the never-ceasing fight with the dirt that is constantly tracked on any farm kitchen floor. Washing clothes for nine people had to be squeezed into the daily routine, too.

Although often tired to the point of exhaustion at bedtime, Daisy rejoiced in her strength and health which enabled her to sleep soundly and wake refreshed, with renewed energy to meet the day's demands. She was determined that the children should be kept neat and well-dressed, the house clean, and the food sanitary, no small feat in Midwestern summer heat without electricity.

She had seen too much carelessness among the hired help during the hectic days before her sister's death. At one end of the cookstove was a storage unit holding water to be used for refilling the teakettle or for washing purposes. Daisy had seen Mrs. Smart, a kindly woman with whose husband Herb had business dealings, give baby Juanita a drink from the reservoir. The water was not at all sanitary for the bottom of the storage unit was lined with dirty chunks of lime and the water there seldom, if ever, boiled.

It was hard to reason with the older girls that water from

the "resevoy," as Herb pronounced it, was unfit to drink. They had done pretty much as they pleased for many months with no adult to guide them except their father and his attention was usually gained only when bad behavior demanded swift punishment. Herb told his sister-in-law that one Saturday soon after the funeral he had come home from town to find Floyd and Carol wrestling in one corner of the kitchen, oblivious to the peril waving arms and legs posed for the table still covered with noon dishes. Grace, the hired girl, unable to restore order, was tearfully peeling potatoes while Jean and Neil danced around gleefully, enjoying the ruckus.

Daisy sighed. In the schoolroom she knew how to deal effectively with such behavior: keep them busy and have the backing of your superiors which, in the World War I era was the cornerstone of well-run classrooms. But here, she was dubious of how her methods would appeal to Herb, used to Myrtie's easy ways. She also knew that her in-laws, who already had made their disapproval of her "schoolteacher ways" apparent, would use any strong action on her part as added fuel for the fire of pity they loudly vocalized for the motherless children.

Herb's sister, Linnie, and her husband, Jim, a prosperous baker in Croquille, were the most irritating thorn in Daisy's side that summer. It seemed to Daisy that Alta, their oldest daughter, a strong, take-charge teenager, devoted too much energy to her motherless cousins.

She recalled with tightened lips the stories Myrtie had told her about the derogatory remarks leveled at her and the children's clothes by the Campbells in an effort, Daisy thought bitterly, to "improve" Herb's wife, who they considered incompetent from too much schooling. Since none of the Nortons had much formal education and all were in comfortable economic circumstances they felt people with college degrees—especially women—were somehow suspect.

When her younger sister had hotly protested such comments on personal matters, Myrtie had quieted her by saying with a sigh, "When you get married, Daisy, you have to get along with your in-laws; what would Herb think if I got the Campbells mad at us?"

Daisy shook her head, remembering painfully Myrtie's beautiful eyes and sweet voice. Yes, she would never tell people to mind their own business. She only complained to her younger sister in private.

But Daisy was different-in-laws be damned, she muttered, as she gave her mop an extra fierce wring, wishing it was Alta's flaming red hair which she had in her hands instead.

Along in mid-August, as if the heat and endless work were not enough to bear, Daisy developed a skin rash over her entire body. She was too proud and reserved to mention it to anyone, let alone her brother-in-law. But Jean's sharp eyes soon detected the cause of her aunt's retiring to her room frequently during the day, and the child promptly informed her father that "Aunt Daidy itches worse than when I had hives."

The next afternoon Daisy, feeling hot and miserable, was sitting in the large front bedroom upstairs that overlooked three stately elm trees in the Mississippi River pasture across the road. She hoped the languid laziness of the floating cumulus clouds and shimmering river would soothe her mind, if not her skin.

She was startled when Herb knocked on her door. "So you have hives-what did you eat, too many strawberries?" he asked in a business-like voice. Without waiting for her to answer and disregarding her blush, he held her arm toward the window and scrutinized it.

"I-oh, it's nothing, really," Daisy at last found her voice. "Probably heat rash, don't you think?" wondering why she needed confirmation of the obvious.

"I have some rubbing alcohol; you better douse yourself with that tonight," Herb continued examining her arm, strong and shapely despite the irritation, as impersonally as if it were the leg of a sick animal.

Not wanting him to think she had been suffering in martyred ignorance, Daisy quickly explained she had a prescription from the little drugstore in Soo Falls, the little town across the river where Herb took his cream and got groceries.

"You don't want any of those fool concoctions." Herb brushed aside her remark as if nothing from a drugstore could possibly be any good.

"Why, it's supposed to be widely used. . . Mr. Babcock said. . ." Daisy began professionally, not used to having people completely ignore her judgment. But Herb muttered scathingly, "Old Charlie would say anything was good if he thought a person would be dumb enough to believe it. I'll give you that alcohol tonight," and with that he turned to go. At the door he smiled, the blue-gray of his eyes becoming as deep blue as the river in the distance, Daisy thought.

"You'll soon get over it; hives usually last only a couple of days," he said reassuringly and was gone.

Daisy, again left alone in her room in the farmhouse after the talk with her brother-in-law, listened thoughtfully to his firm tread until the slam of the screen door told her he had left the house. The last time they had talked alone she had been the one to be reassuring. She was startled to recall how glibly she had offered words of comfort then. Now, after two months of living in his house and caring for his children, she felt inadequate to offer advice and any attempt to talk with him caused her to feel strangely reticent.

Never having been in similar circumstances before, she had no precedent to guide her actions and she found her old shyness and reserve filling the gap of uncertainty. She was in the odd position where she was neither hired girl nor wife. Delicacy constrained her from offering profuse sympathy. Judging by her own feelings, she thought the most appreciated policy she could pursue in the face of another's personal grief was respectful silence.

She felt cooler and much more peaceful after Herb's visit, impersonal and brief as it had been. There was something calming about his brisk, efficient manner. But why, she wondered, was he so prejudiced about pharmaceutical remedies? It seemed rather silly to her to discredit something before one had time to give it a fair trial. Perhaps he hadn't really meant anything and his remark about the drugstore owner was an expression of grumbling affection common to farmers who hate to show any sign of emotion. Herb, she was learning, was prone to make rash statements about people or issues "off the top of his head" without any serious thought. If he were closely questioned about them-and farmers usually need not verify their opinions-often there would be no rational reason.

3

Harvest time brought the usual interchange of crews for silo filling and threshing. This meant ten to fifteen men to prepare meals for, meals where the emphasis was not on style, or the kind of salad served-indeed the men would have snorted at salad-but on hearty, filling food. Oceans of potatoes, gravy, meat, and baked beans were needed to satisfy the tall, lanky German Catholic neighbors with whom Herb exchanged harvest work.

With all the agitation about German Americans during the Great War, Daisy was eager to study these farmers-typical German stock whose fathers or grandfathers had come from the "old country" (as they always referred to Europe) to homestead farms in central Minnesota. They worked hard and, except for the sense of community provided by the Catholic Church, mostly forgot ethnic traditions.

Daisy, having the tolerance that should always accompany education (but unfortunately does not) entertained none of the animosity for those of German blood that was common during the recent war. She had lived with a lovely cultured German family in Goose Lake and realized the fallaciousness of the contention that an entire nationality was evil.

But as she watched the dull features of the men, brightened

only by the appearance of more food, and listened to their accent while they discussed crops and weather and gossiped about other neighbors, Daisy realized sharply the vast distance between the cultured and the uneducated. She pitied these men with scarcely four or five years of schooling, kept home as soon as they were old enough to help on the farm, to whom politics, let alone literature or economic theories, meant nothing.

Despite the relatives' prediction that the "citified" schoolteacher would be overcome at the prospect of feeding harvest crews, Daisy, by planning her menus in advance, directed preparations and served without a flaw the meals and lunches which the farmers expected. But her indignation rose at the insistence from Max Traut, boss of the crew, that not only mid-afternoon lunch be served, but also a morning snack around 10 A.M. It was impossible to get the morning work done, make the sandwiches and coffee the men thought they needed, and still prepare the noon meal on time.

If the harvest crew began working at dawn they would have a right to be hungry by mid-forenoon, Daisy reasoned, but the men seldom arrived before nine, after doing their own chores. They were just getting well started pitching the heavy green bundles of corn off the wagons into the cutter where sharp knives cut the stalks into silage and blower pipes forced it to the top of the silo where it fell like thick hail into the dusky pit, when the whole operation had to stop for the morning repast. It was ridiculous.

"Herb, we just can't serve lunch in the morning, too. It's a tight squeeze to finish the dishes and get dinner," she complained to her brother-in-law one evening as he was gathering milk pail, strainer, and empty milk cans to depart for the evening milking.

Always attentive to her comfort, Herb listened seriously to her heated argument about the folly of having two between-meal lunches.

"All right, I'll speak to Max," he said as he strode toward the homely red barn where all his evenings were spent. Daisy, working in the kitchen now silent after the clamor of family supper, felt rather guilty that she had argued so forcibly. She had expected him to disagree and was surprised that he could appreciate her situation.

She reflected on his attitude while she rinsed the plates prior to washing them-just like washing them twice, her nieces scoffingly told her. Hearing childish voices from the hayfield, she smiled. There is something mysteriously invigorating about new mown hay. Even the third crop in September holds the same fascination as does the first one in June. To children its fragrance tantalizes the senses, making them want to run, jump over, and leap into the soft bunches. The beauty of waving grain, the smell of fresh clover-these are the fond memories of farm children, offsetting, at least for some, the tediousness of hard physical labor.

Watching the children scurry and leap over the windrows, their aunt was thankful for their pleasure with the offerings of nature, besides relieved to be alone. She found that, more than the hard work, the never-ceasing activity of the household which gave her no privacy from the minute she arose until she retired, wore on her nerves. Often after supper she would tell the older girls to go outdoors to play, glad to do the dishes in peace.

She could not help but entertain a feeling of satisfaction in her efforts during the summer, for despite all obstacles the children were together and in good health.

Floyd and Carol were in school that fall, driving to Soo Falls with horse and buggy. Daisy was surprised that Herb would allow his nine-year-old child to drive across the bridge and railroad tracks into town, but Herb was proud of his tall older son and saw nothing disturbing about the two starting off, their heads hidden by the tall buggy seat. Someday that boy will make a good farmer, Herb thought fondly, noticing the skill with which his son managed old Sam, the patient saddle horse.

As Christmas drew near, Daisy worked long hours after the children were in bed, sewing doll clothes, and fixing fancy candy boxes for each child. She found that farm income was stretched to the breaking point by the time groceries, clothes, and the seasonal machinery repairs were purchased. Quietly, she used her own money to add extra dainties for the holidays.

Herb had been used to treating his wife as a partner in their financial affairs, with the mutual understanding that whichever one happened to take the cream into town would then cash and spend the check, which was always modest. He saw no reason for handing the woman a certain amount of money, as he knew his German neighbors did, when she knew as well as he what was needed. And he felt no need to change this habit with Daisy; after all, he reflected, she was sensible and had handled her own money and should know what they needed.

While he had been perfectly happy with his first wife, who had been a competent homemaker, her constant habit of tardiness had often irritated him. Daisy, he noticed, seemed much better organized. If he took the cream to town, Daisy made the grocery list, putting at the last such luxuries as fruit to be bought only if there was money left after essentials. If she took it, he told her if farm supplies were needed.

Since she had always enjoyed cooking, before the older children were home for Christmas vacation Daisy had oatmeal cookies, graham bread, date cake, and sour cream cookies stowed away in the large pantry which extended across one end of the kitchen.

Christmas always brings a bustle of excitement and work, especially when there are children in the household. To the youngsters, the flurry of mysterious packages, boxes, and action may seem Santa's doing, but adults who have helped the jolly fellow know that every child's joy must be preceded by hard work. Daisy was truly thankful to be able to take such an active part in making a happy Christmas for the motherless children.

It was an annual source of wonder to her to watch people visibly become kinder and more generous as December rolled around. Why shouldn't they be that way all the time, she wondered, or if they weren't sincere, they shouldn't be such hypocrites, she privately moralized.

Whether sincere or not, the entire Norton household radiated seasonal good will. Christmas day dawned cold, but sunny. After the breakfast dishes were finished and the morning farm chores completed, the children trooped happily into the parlor to distribute their presents. Daisy was touched by the tokens of affection they gave her and treasured them more than if they had been expensive purchases. Carol had made a hot pad in school and Jean, with the help of her older sister, had picked out a pincushion for her aunt. The boys had made her a woven basket.

For once, Herb was in the house during the day and it was pleasant to see him playing with his children again. There was no rest for Daisy for as soon as the wrappings were cleared away, she began the holiday dinner, setting the long table with its leaves stretched to capacity, bringing out pies, cakes, and cookies and fixing the individual fruit salads artistically. Their aunt was determined that they would have one meal served in civilized manner, with butter knives, napkins, and separate courses.

It was after four o'clock when the kitchen work was done and Daisy sank wearily into the rocker in the sitting room, looking forward to a well-deserved evening's rest watching the children enjoy their new gifts. Then she would light the candles on the tree and let the children enjoy them while she carefully guarded against fire danger.

Suddenly the telephone sounded the family's signal on the party line-three short and one long ring. Alta Campbell wanted to know if Herb couldn't bring the "kiddies" down to their house in town for the evening so they could enjoy their tree and all the decorations. Daisy bristled inwardly at her blithe insinuation that there was nothing special at the farmhouse in the way of decorations or holiday atmosphere.

It was on the tip of Daisy's tongue to refuse but it was Herb's business and the children thought it wonderful to go to the nicely furnished Campbell house in town. Their father obligingly agreed to drive them the three miles with team and sled, so Daisy dutifully started helping them get dressed.

She had been so occupied with cooking, cleaning, and making presents during the past weeks that she had had no time to ready a holiday outlay of clothes for each child, expecting them to be at home Christmas day. She was vexed that the Campbells would have an opportunity to shake their heads in the "just-what-I-told-you" manner. But the children, oblivious to whether their clothes were old or new, joyously piled into the sleigh and with a tinkle of bells, the team was off.

Silently Daisy turned back into the empty house to spend the remainder of Christmas alone.

4

The heart has reasons that reason does not understand.
— *Bossuet*

During the long winter months when the roads were blocked with snow, making it impossible to leave the farm, Daisy became aware of the desolation and complete obscurity from civilization which farm residents experience. How could one live shut off from all the cultural benefits of city life, she wondered.

Used to seeing an occasional stage play and hearing authoritative speakers discuss world affairs, she missed such events, although she never had considered them intellectual, just a way of life.

But she was too busy to miss city life intensely, although the change from a modern apartment to the seven-room farmhouse, heated by wood stoves, with no plumbing or electricity, was rather disconcerting. Daisy didn't mind for herself, but she worried about her mother. Flora Jane maintained her cheerfulness but because of her total deafness, she seemed rather a pitiful and detached figure to her grandchildren. The only way to communicate with her was to write and children are too restless to take time to write out their scampering thoughts.

To Daisy, however, caring for her mother was a labor of love of which she never tired. Since she was the youngest of her large family and the only one without a family of her own, it was only natural that it should fall upon her to care for her mother after her father, a Civil War veteran, had decided to move to Arkansas. Besides, Ma had wanted to live with her youngest daughter rather than traipse off down South where Pa probably would provide only some old hut, Daisy reasoned. The warmth of her love melted any effect of the caustic remarks of less sentimental observers that her family simply had left the job of supporting the old lady to Daisy.

There had been talk among her older brothers, who were less idealistic than Daisy, that their father's apparent abandonment of his family, albeit the children were all grown, had some connection with a lady friend in whose company he reportedly left. But if Daisy had heard the gossip, she would have immediately denied it. After all, she told friends, her father's health had been impaired while a prisoner of the Confederates and the warmer climate was better for him.

That winter, Juanita, who turned two, was seriously ill with an ear infection and Daisy, staying up nights to watch her, wondered bleakly if all there was in life was sickness and people to be served. Service to others, being a good steward of one's God-given abilities-this phase of Christian living had been emphasized by the Methodist Episcopal small rural church where she had grown up, she recalled. And with that thought, her midnight vigil musings veered to memories of Epworth League institutes and a summer camp meet she had once attended at Lake Geneva.

The memory of that companionship with inspirational leaders and consecrated Christians always produced an invigorating effect on her. No matter how long the intervening years, youthful religious experiences leave a stronger influence than sophisticated adults often realize. And thinking of these things, the long nights passed. Juanita recovered and again entertained her older brothers and sisters with her chubby smile. A darling baby, was the consensus of the whole family. As the weather warmed, Daisy would bundle her up and, with Neil to watch her, send the two youngsters into the big yard to play.

With the first appearance of bare ground, Daisy sensed Herb's eagerness to begin the spring planting. The feeling of reawakening, when bitter winter storms are forgotten and hopes for a good harvest are sown along with the sweat and seed-these were the almost unconscious sensations Herb, like farmers for centuries, experienced every spring, ever since he had helped on his father's farm as a boy.

He would have laughed self-consciously at the comparison to an architect mingling love and skill with his plans for stone and bricks, yet much more than a shiny plow shear turned over the glistening black loam on his land, for the spirit was in his work.

Watching him trudge behind the plow, often walking to lighten the horses' burden, Daisy thought of Browning's description of the man who "once putting his hand to the plow, did not turn back." She, too, sensed the thrill of nature's awakening and rejoiced that the confinement of snow-blocked roads was over.

At mealtime Herb was full of plans and Daisy found herself hoping as anxiously as he that a late March freeze would not impede the grain planting. Often at night, after the children were in bed, they would linger in the kitchen to discuss the weather and seeding.

"If the good weather holds I can get the back field plowed and the grain in by April first," Herb explained.

"That's April Fool's Day-no joking about it," Daisy laughingly replied. Grinning at her merry tone, Herb repeated the old rhyme,

"April Fool's a coming

And you're the biggest fool a'running."

"I know that one too," she cried, completing the jingle:

"April Fool's gone and past

And you're the biggest fool at last."

Then adding softly, glancing at her brother-in-law, "I don't mean that personally."

"Well, I'm glad you don't," Herb replied. Serious now, he looked thoughtfully at Daisy and said softly, "You know I need you here."

Daisy, who had long wished to hear such words, now found herself suddenly worried. "What will the children think?" she asked, breaking their happy rapport.

"I guess you'll just have to ask them," Herb responded. It was a sensible answer, but the question had now become only a practical one.

"We'd better hope this warm spell continues and the horses get used to hard work after their winter rest," Herb easily switched back to his workaday concerns. "If it just doesn't get too warm for them . . ." he said, his propensity to borrow trouble easily surfacing. She had had no idea of the vital importance the weather played for Midwestern farmers, even though she had grown up in the country.

Her father had been a "farmer of sorts," as Herb often said

privately, having learned not to criticize his father-in-law in Myrtice's hearing.

"Your Grandpa Coolidge would sit up half the night reading some fool book, then lie abed in the morning instead of taking care of things," Herb would tell his sons.

There was no resemblance in the vigorous schedule Herb maintained to the haphazard management on the much smaller Coolidge farm years earlier. But equally as important as Herb's diligence was the gamble of the weather, with his children's livelihood at stake.

There was little sleep for the schoolteacher these spring nights. Was it that intangible called spring fever, or the shoptalk Herb shared with her that banished sleep and troubled her dreams with episodes that seemed proof of Freudian theories?

She felt herself in the grip of forces which neither her mind nor hand could stay, leaving her helpless to do anything but turn and toss restlessly. It would be hard-veritably a cross, without exaggeration-if she would follow the promptings of her heart. Her mind rebelled; her hard-earned education and training had been gained for better use than to "lie in cold obstruction and to rot."

Struggling with her feelings, she knelt one night by the big window in her bedroom overlooking the three elms in the Mississippi River pasture. The scene always satisfied and calmed her. Now by moonlight it looked mysterious and romantic. Romance; the word made her start. "Dear God, let me think clearly now," she whispered.

There was no question about it; she was needed, Herb had said so. Yet, could she do it? When a troubled Daisy had written out her uneasy thoughts to her mother, she had been told, "You can't stand it, Daisy. No woman could take this job with the hard work and five children and come out alive." But I'm strong, thought Daisy, I can stand it.

This was her last chance to escape. If she wanted to go back to the cities, now was the time, when next year's teaching contracts were being signed. No, escape wasn't the word. She seemed drawn and held as if by a magnet to this family. Was it love? Love for her beloved dead sister and the motherless children? Or another kind of love? It was one thing to be needed; another to be loved.

How could she live with herself, knowing that she had fled back to the comforts of a teacher's life because she was afraid? Afraid-not of the poverty and hard work—but of jealousy and suspicion, the barrier of the memory of her sister which held her, as if by an invisible hand, on the perimeter of the heart of the family which she had loved for so long.

She leaned her burning forehead against the cool windowpane and tears filled her eyes, making them glow with the light of a peace which flooded her being. Better to lose trying, than not to attempt high things, an oft repeated literary theme, ran through her mind.

Satisfied with her decision and relieved to end the uncertainty, with a murmured prayer for strength, she wearily rose from her knees. As she moved from the window where the moonlight and the intensity of her meditation had lifted her thoughts above mundane perplexities, her glow of emotion was rudely shattered as she thought of the personal situation she faced with her brother-in-law.

It was one thing to conquer one's own selfishness; mastering personal negative emotions she had trained herself to do. But could she ever feel really loved in her own right when her brother-in-law had been so happily married to Myrtie? She wondered if any deep relationship could be developed with Herb or if it would just be a marriage of convenience.

Too weary to contemplate another problem, she hugged her pillow to her tightly and could not dispel the feeling that such matters would take care of themselves. With a tired but happy sigh, she slept soundly for the first time in weeks.

Several nights later as she was tucking the girls into bed in the corner of her own bedroom, she asked in a low voice, "How would you like to have me for your Mama?" The sleepy children, little realizing the anguish with which she awaited their reaction, were at once awake, filled with curiosity.

"You mean stay here always?" Carol asked, her eyes wide with astonishment, while Jean, for whom the memory of her mother already had faded, threw her arms around Daisy impulsively crying, "Goody, now we'll have a real mother like the other kids." Unnerved by her bland assumption that she would be able to take Myrtice's place, her aunt was glad to hide her face in Jean's blond hair.

Hearing the word "mother" repeated, Juanita murmured the name into the grateful ears of the only woman the child could remember.

"Will you marry Dad?" Carol, with all the worldly wisdom gained from one year of public school, realized at once her aunt's unique position. Her bluntness made her aunt shiver.

"We'll talk about that later, you'd better get settled to sleep now," and with a good-night kiss, Daisy fled from the room wondering if she had gained or lost in her first move in the delicate tangle she faced.

5

As the spring days wore into early summer, the news buzzed over the fence posts in the rural neighborhood: Herb Norton was going to marry his schoolteacher sister-in-law. The old German farmers shook their heads-"Too high-falutin' to make a good farmer's wife," was their opinion. The women, considering the Nortons with the reserve that good Catholics view Protestant activity, especially marriages, looked upon Daisy as an alien, both in religion and background.

Having nothing in common with her and feeling inferior because of her college degree, which they believed made her look down on them, the neighbor women simply ignored Daisy. They worked hard and had little free time to socialize but if she had been of their church, there would have been the unspoken bond and socializing inherit in any church fellowship.

She, in turn, while pitying their narrow lives, and not knowing how to talk with them, found her old shyness being covered by a reserve which was perceived as haughty.

But the lack of neighborliness among farmers whose buildings could be seen from each others' fields, was only a mental situation which had little practical effect upon Daisy, for preparation for her wedding now consumed all her time. She was determined to have a nice ceremony, the kind to which one invites all the relatives and can remember with pleasure the rest of one's life.

However, marrying a man with five children, even in a simple home ceremony, she discovered, was no easy project. Everyone had to be outfitted with new clothes, including Grandma, who received a new white dress, made by her daughter's nimble fingers.

Besides the sewing, there was baking, cleaning, sending handwritten invitations in her distinctive penmanship to all the brothers and sisters on each side of the family. Weddings, like most good things in life, require much hard work, the bride-to-be learned.

She also found that making the girls' new dresses was easy compared to buying a suit for Floyd. The boy, shy and diffident, would start crying whenever Daisy got him into a store. Baffled and at a loss as to how to cope with her nephew, she decided to turn this problem over to his father.

When Herb demanded the reason for the tears, Floyd haltingly expressed his fear of being abandoned again, an idea which his father soundly denounced, completely ignoring his son's childish interpretation of his mother's death.

"No one is going anywhere," Herb said. "We're all staying right here and working," he added, more to himself though as he thought fleetingly that it was hardly a fitting start for his new wife. It was the last time he ever knew Floyd's thoughts.

The wedding day, June 20, 1920, was blessed with the best of June weather; the children, excited and thrilled with their new clothes and seeing so many cousins, enjoyed the unusual holiday atmosphere. The refreshments, all of which had been prepared by the bride, looked and tasted excellent.

If the guests had any reservations about this marriage, so obviously one of convenience for Herb and his children, they said nothing to mar the gathering.

But the tacit disapproval of Daisy's own family was obvious. Only one of her five siblings attended-Sid, the most erratic brother who, like another sibling, Gene, was a struggling farmer near Elk Grove.

The six Norton siblings all came, even Fred who farmed in the northern part of the state.

Daisy's only remaining sister, Eva, the oldest of the clan, apparently wanted to let her know that she could never replace Myrtice, Daisy thought bitterly. Myrtie had always been Eva's favorite and while Daisy felt strong family loyalty, she never was truly comfortable with her oldest sister whose sharp tongue so contrasted with Myrtice's gentle ways. Perhaps Floy, the third sister who had died at age twenty-eight of tuberculosis, would have been more understanding.

Daisy momentarily thought about how ironic life is. She had lost both sisters who were such comforts, leaving only Eva who, it seemed, was not going to support her in this major step. But then, Daisy thought, Eva had never had the pleasure of even a simple home wedding for she had run off with her happy-go-lucky Bill in defiance of her father who had forbidden the marriage.

Robbie, the brother who lived out West, of course couldn't be expected to come, and both Bret and Gene Coolidge's wives had written tactful notes explaining their absence. Since no word had come from Eva, Daisy felt sure she would arrive, bustling and expecting to take charge of the kitchen, no doubt.

As the hour for the ceremony neared and she realized that only one of her own family had cared enough to come, hot anger filled Daisy's already weary body. However, with long practice of self-discipline, she soon recovered her composure and decided to ask Sid and his pleasant wife, Anna, to act as witnesses. Because of the circumstances and age of the bridal pair, there were no attendants, but at least she would have some from her own family sign the lovely wedding book she had so proudly purchased.

Before the assembled Norton relatives, Herb and Daisy stood with the minister in front of the parlor window looking out on the Mississippi River pasture and took vows "till death do us part." Daisy shuddered, thinking what that phrase must evoke in her husband's mind.

As the guests began leaving after enjoying refreshments, Sid and Anna offered to take Jean and Carol home with them for a week, to give the new bride a breather. The Campbells took the two boys home with them. This left only baby Juanita, now two and a half, and Grandma Coolidge, both of whom retired early. At last the newlyweds had a little time to themselves.

So when the milking and other chores were done that evening, Herb and his new bride took a walk in the June twilight. Daisy laughingly referred later to that stroll to the pasture which bordered the Soo River as their "honeymoon trip," characteristically making no comment on what emotions were expressed.

While the daily work routine continued unabated, for Daisy everything had changed. She was now married to the man she had long secretly loved. But years of repressing her feelings and now the continued need for tact in memory of the person for whom they both still grieved, helped her maintain her usual reserve.

She found her relationship with the children little changed; the two older girls seemed glad to have a "real mother," and the two youngest were too small for the marriage to have any significance. Only Floyd, who had long been her favorite nephew, continued aloof and withdrawn but she was too occupied to brood over his rejection of her. She could understand his insistence on continuing to call her Aunt Daisy, as he was old enough to keenly feel his own mother's death. But, even though he obviously could not accept her as a replacement, Daisy thought exasperatedly, why couldn't they still be friends as in past years?

During her years as the old maid schoolteacher in the large Coolidge clan she had spent many weeks during summer vacations visiting Myrtie's family. She also had stayed long periods with her brother, Gene, who like their father, scraped out a living farming. While there she made clothes for his large family. During those past summers, which now seemed idyllic compared to her present responsibilities, Daisy often took pictures with her Kodak box camera and one year on Myrtie's birthday she had given her sister a photo album, in which she had affixed many of these snapshots of Floyd, Carol, and Jean and their cousins when they were small.

Coming across the album one day in her cleaning, Daisy had looked at it fondly, vowing to keep on taking snapshots to record the years while the five little Nortons were growing up.

Even though she had no contact with neighbors and only cursory contact with church members when she attended the Methodist services in Croquille, Daisy's days were full, caring for the five children and operating the large household where work was more difficult without what are known as modern conveniences. Herb's farming and sideline business activities provided the only variety to life.

One day she took snapshots of all the youngsters in various

poses in front of Herb's 1917 Chevrolet, with Floyd persuaded to hold little Juanita, demure in a pretty lace cap. Even though Floyd never warmed to her, Daisy enjoyed pleasant evenings watching while he played with the pet cat she had brought from St. Paul. Whimsically named Nicodemus Beelzebub by his doting mistress, the cat would thrash his way out from under an open newspaper Floyd placed over him. He tore the paper to shreds, but Daisy didn't complain, glad to have her nephew seemingly happy.

That summer Herb brought home a small pup of presumed shepherd breed and the children played and fought over him all day. That first night, during a heavy rain, when Daisy heard him crying in the shed where Herb, with a farmer's stoical attitude toward pets, had firmly put him for the night, she ran out in her nightgown and brought the poor shivering pup into the warmth of the kitchen.

After that, she could call Jack, as he was finally named, to her from any of the children, as he seemed to never forget that early kindness. But she seldom tried to show her power over the dog, glad to see the children romping with him in the fresh air.

When school started that fall Daisy felt comfortable making herself known at Russell Grade School, an old brick Romanesque structure in Soo Falls, across the river. The three-story building had two wings, one of which housed the high school and the other the grade school, with a wide corridor connecting the two. This hallway also included a classroom where the students were often distracted by anyone passing through the connecting hall on errands.

After introducing herself as a fellow educator, Daisy quickly became friends with each of the three older children's teachers. She soon decided that the high school was most inadequate and vowed, silently, that when Floyd graduated from eighth grade, he should transfer to the much better equipped high school in Croquille.

In an effort to do something perhaps helpful for her nieces and Floyd, as well as provide a little social life which she and Herb lacked, having no friends as a couple, Daisy invited the three teachers for an evening on the farm that winter. She prevailed upon Herb to hitch the team to the hayrack on runners which served as winter transportation and take them for a sleigh ride, after which she served oyster stew and hot cocoa in the big farm kitchen. This she continued yearly while all five children were in school.

Jean, especially, thought this was a nice thing for her aunt to do-though she called Daisy Mama as did all the other children except Floyd.

"It makes us seem a little special to our teachers," she told Carol one cold morning as they were striding off on the mile walk to school.

"And it gives Mama a little company, too," Carol replied. "She hardly ever goes anywhere and they seldom have any company."

"Except Campbells and she doesn't seem to like them." Jean laughed, too young to appreciate that Daisy, despite her college degree, felt insecure with her in-laws, mostly because she sensed their critical attitude.

The girls shook their heads, as if indicating there was nothing they could do to change their new mother's life, though they vaguely realized she was doing all she could to care for them.

The teachers were not sparkling intellectuals, yet education always provides a broad blanket for sharing concern and fertile ideas for conversation. For Daisy, it was like a breath of fresh air.

However, since the sleigh ride meant that Herb had to milk the Holsteins early-a break in routine upon which he frowned-Daisy realized that the once-a-year social event was about all she could expect. Fortunately, a former school chum from her hometown now taught in the teachers' college in Croquille and occasionally she enjoyed stimulating visits with Blanch Atkins, who had never married.

She limped on a twisted foot resulting from infantile paralysis as a child, but, as Herb cheerfully said, "Blanch may be crippled in her foot, but not in her head." Daisy feared he would resent much contact with the brilliant, highly-opinionated educator, but there was not time for enough visiting to create problems.

The next year after her marriage, Daisy realized her mother's health was failing. Indeed, the grandchildren thought secretly of her as half-dead already since she seemed content to sit complacently, a lace cap covering her mostly bald head, and watch the busy household around her with a placid smile.

"When your grandmother got to be 65, she just folded her hands and gave up," was Herb's opinion of his mother-in-law, delivered frequently out of Daisy's hearing to any listening child. As she got feebler, Herb had to lift the old lady from wheelchair into bed at night and out in the morning.

One Saturday night, on his weekly trip to the barbershop in Soo Falls, the regular customers, who enjoyed the easy camaraderie of any group which sees each other often, asked why he walked all stooped over. Had he fallen and hurt himself?

"Just lifting my mother-in-law, who seems like a sack of flour," he told them. A few nights later, hearing a noise in Flora Jane's bedroom, Herb came downstairs to find her somehow on her feet, stuffing papers into the stove.

Upon his inquiry as to what on earth she was doing, the old woman replied that she was "just getting rid of things so you won't have so much to do when I'm gone." A few weeks later she was dead, shortly before her seventy-sixth birthday. And once again, two years after her daughter's funeral there, the Coolidge relatives gathered in the Norton parlor.

Bret, who was a schoolteacher in St. Paul, as Daisy had been, seemed particularly upset over her death. Herb found it difficult to be impressed by his apparent grief, for he had visited his mother only once a year, bringing her a small sack of peppermint candy each time. This seemingly innocuous gesture had prompted Herb more than once to remark, "Well, Bret has spent his yearly ten cents on his mother's support."

Herb figured he himself probably was a little better off financially than either of Daisy's two brothers who were marginal farmers. But since Bret had a regular salary, not dependent upon the vagaries of weather, Herb blithely assumed his brother-in-law was rich, not realizing the teacher's paycheck was stretched thin to support his wife and three children in the city.

Just as Daisy's siblings had taken for granted that she would support her mother, once she married, it was also assumed that Herb would shoulder the financial obligation. And while what Grandma had eaten was scarcely significant, it only proved what most adults eventually learn: in every large family there are usually many who avoid responsibility for their parents, and always one who somehow assumes it.

As Herb often put it in his pithy dissertations delivered while pitching hay or other repetitious jobs requiring no mental concentration (a practice which drove Floyd crazy but intrigued Neil), "There are two kinds of people in this world; those who are willing to work and those who are willing to let them."

6

Although Daisy missed her mother's silent support, she had to admit that her demise resulted in more adequate sleeping arrangements. She and Herb now took the downstairs bedroom, allowing Jean and Carol to move into the big front upstairs bedroom from the smaller one on the south which all three girls had shared.

The household now narrowed to just the children and their father and stepmother/aunt. Herb decided he could get along without the help of the hired man. The hired girl, who had tried vainly to keep order after Myrtice's death, had left some time ago for a more lucrative job in town.

Daisy was content to have them gone, though it meant even more housework. When she had arrived on the farm in the spring of 1919, the kitchen did not have a "wet sink"-the colloquialism for sinks having a drain. This meant carrying out all water used for domestic purposes in the well-named slop bucket.

Herb had remedied this inconvenience by hiring a man to dig a cesspool and install a drain for the large sink. Daisy hoped someday something could be done about the outhouse which was embarrassingly obvious. It was in plain view of anyone driving into the large farmyard, or open area separating the house, well, and water tank from the large two-story barn which housed the horses and cattle.

Although she mentally was determined to not only run the house efficiently but have flowers and a garden, after a few months Daisy reluctantly agreed when Herb scolded her solicitously for trying to care for flowers.

"You've got too much to do inside; Myrtice never even tried to have flowers," he told her. Someday, she thought, when the children were older and left home, she'd be glad to have a nicely landscaped lawn, the idea of her ready-made family ever being grown suddenly putting her heavy workload in perspective. Meanwhile, she settled for sweet peas in a bed which Herb thoughtfully had built for her, stringing woven wire between two sturdy posts he pounded into the ground near the clothes-line on what could loosely be called a lawn. She knew this was his way of expressing his gratitude and growing affection.

The kitchen garden, of course, was not a frill but a necessity. The fresh vegetables helped in the summer and the canned ones, along with potatoes, pumpkin, and squash stored in bins in the cellar under the house, were a mainstay during winter.

Through Herb's diligent work planting, cultivating, and harvesting his crops and year-round daily care of his dairy cows and workhorses, as well as a small flock of sheep and a few pigs, along with prudent spending on Daisy's part, they were able to clothe and feed their family. But there never was enough money for the slightest luxury, or clothes, or medical care. The occasional extra cash coming from the sale of wool when the sheep were sheared each spring, or shipping lambs to the stockyards in South St. Paul, went for major items such as shoes, a constant need with five youngsters.

Daisies Don't Tell

One hot summer day Daisy was pinning up the hem on a dress she was making for Carol. She had the girl standing atop the kitchen table so the hemline would be at a convenient level while she sat. With her head high above what little breeze came through the windows, the girl fainted from the excessive heat.

Herb, happening in from his fieldwork at that unfortunate minute and seeing Carol lying on the floor where Daisy had laid her after she slumped down on the table, shouted hysterically, "What's the matter with her? She looks just like Myrtice."

Daisy, already disconcerted by Carol's fainting, was further disturbed by Herb's reference to Myrtice. She supposed seeing the girl lying still reminded him of how her mother had looked, lying comatose for several weeks before her death.

She quietly sprinkled cold water on the prone girl, calmly assuring her father that she had just become too warm up near the ceiling. Carol quickly recovered and Daisy finished pinning the hem with the dress spread out on the table, as she had a good eye for straight lines.

The incident, so easily explained physically, nevertheless left a lasting worry in Daisy's mind. How would Herb ever cope if something did happen to any of his children, she wondered. She decided his somewhat superstitious nature had been unduly aroused by the likeness of the still form to her mother, which apparently was not noticeable while Carol pursued normal activity.

She recalled his telling her about hearing a loon cry the first spring he had moved to the farm-unusual for that part of the state. He apparently connected it to his first wife's death, Daisy realized.

Her more disciplined mind naturally rejected such premonitions and she soon had more positive thoughts of the future, for she realized she was pregnant. Herb, knowing well the expense of feeding and clothing children, had not been keen on adding to his family, but he knew it was Daisy's fond dream to have a child of her own, and his, so he was happy for her.

She soon was spending every spare minute sewing delicate baby clothes which, as a special treat, she would allow the children to gaze upon occasionally as she lovingly arranged her layette in a bureau drawer. She ordered several maternity dresses from Lane Bryant. By mistake, the mail order firm sent them to Mrs. Irvin Norton, the wife of Herb's younger brother, who also had an account with them. When this congenial lady, Alta Norton, got the package and brought it out to the farm, accompanied by Linnie Campbell, they were chagrined to find that the expectant mother was "not at home."

Daisy was so annoyed with the mix-up that allowed the Norton clan to know of her condition long before she wanted it to be known, that she refused to come downstairs to see them.

The women, who were enjoying private snickers about thus learning that their somewhat remote sister-in-law was "in the family way," had expected to inflict a little good-natured ribbing. However, with no one to talk to but the children, they soon left.

Carol, by now a mature twelve years, felt embarrassed about her stepmother's seeming petulance but Jean, aware of Daisy's pride and reticence, felt sorry about the incident.

As the spring of 1923 arrived, so did the anticipation of the new arrival in the Norton household. Herb, sensing that Daisy was apprehensive about a first birth at her age (she would be thirty-nine by the expected May delivery) suggested that she take a brief vacation from the farm and visit Connie Rempel, a dear friend from her teaching days in St. Paul.

But Daisy didn't want to go in her present awkward condition. "I'll wait until the baby's big enough to travel and then show him-or her-off," she told Herb happily. He nodded, fervently hoping, as he resumed spring plowing, that nothing would go wrong.

Myrtice had delivered all her children at home without any problem and home delivery was routine, so he saw nothing questionable about the doctor's plans to attend Daisy at home.

But too late, it developed that avoiding hospitalization, and thus added expense, was a tragic mistake, for Daisy developed uremic poisoning. After a long and painful labor in the upstairs bedroom where she had retreated with her first contractions, the doctor, who finally arrived after Herb's frantic phone calls, shook his head.

"They can't both live," he told Herb. "Who do you want to save, your wife or the child?" The brutal question, so cruelly forced on him without the slightest warning or tact, infuriated Herb, his anger momentarily overriding his grief. Asking him to decide was the Catholic influence, he knew; silently thanking God that the birth had not occurred in the Catholic hospital in town. There he would have had no choice; every new soul was needed to spread the faith.

"Who do you think, you idiot?" he nearly shouted at the flustered doctor. "For God's sake, don't let my wife die." His voice trailed off into almost a wail. Not another death in this house, he thought.

There is a saying that a house is not home until a birth, death, and wedding all have taken place within its walls. This house, of all the several farmhouses in which he had lived, had experienced all three events, but too many deaths. This was the third one within four years.

But he soon forgot such musings in trying to comfort Daisy, exhausted physically and crushed to her very core emotionally.

The baby, a beautifully formed girl, already named Ada Beryl, was a pretty infant, her features unaffected by the fate which decreed she was not to experience human life.

This time only the immediate family gathered in the parlor for a brief funeral service. Neither of the parents had the heart, nor the energy, to contact relatives. The children momentarily were disappointed not to have a new baby to brighten their home, but by the time Daisy felt well enough to come downstairs and resume her regular routine, they were outside happily playing and shouting, seemingly immune to her grief.

Daisy shuddered and went back to bed.

7

Daily life does not wait for broken hearts to mend, and in the unending demands of her large family, Daisy soon was seemingly working as usual. But life seemed desolate and sour to her and the children's rowdiness and noise, which previously she had realized was normal, now grated upon her nerves.

She also found she tired much easier now, which she attributed to not yet recovering from childbirth, but she also suspected her grief affected her nerves which often seemed at the breaking point.

Once when Herb came upon her yelling almost hysterically at the children, he quietly suggested she come over to the meadow across the river where he was putting up hay, where she could at least sit in the shade of the trees along the edge and have quiet.

Daisy had taught herself to drive the spring before she was married, mastering the mechanics of backing and shifting the new model Chevrolet Herb had purchased that year. When she felt proficient enough, she told Neil and Juanita to stand in the yard and watch and she would drive out the long farm driveway, up the country road to where another road veered off, turn around at the intersection, and return home. Neil admired her ability and was proud of the trust she placed in him, to be responsible for watching his little sister while the older three children were in school.

So now Daisy felt comfortable driving the car anywhere, and she spent the next afternoon in the shade along the meadow, with the unspoken but visible comfort of Herb working in the distance. She sat and leaned against a tree and relaxed, thanking God for Herb's concern for her. When she returned to the farm, she found the children happily playing "school" with the frogs in a small pond in the sheep pasture, aptly called the frog pond. They made the frogs stand up on their hind legs and give speeches, Jean explained to Daisy, who breathed a prayer of thankfulness for the creativity of children. The children were all expected to work-the boys outside and the girls in the house-but they still eked out some free time for play which is every child's right.

Gypsies often came through the countryside summers, no longer roaming afoot, but in old cars. They often asked to camp in Herb's pasture along the Mississippi River, which had a considerable number of fairly flat spaces under the trees. Daisy kept the screen doors hooked during their stay for she accepted the widely held belief that gypsies would steal anything. They often came to the barn at night when Herb was milking, asking for warm milk which he obligingly gave them.

One gypsy lady, apparently sensing Daisy's ability as a seamstress, asked her to hem a skirt. Daisy felt she had enough to do and was not enthusiastic about assuming the job, but the gypsy finally convinced her to do it. The skirt was so voluminous, it took her several hours of much needed spare time, even though she was an expert seamstress.

"I hate to take the time for it, but since I promised her, I must do it," Daisy told her nieces. They snickered privately that the gypsy had in a sense outwitted their aunt, but they also absorbed her integrity in keeping a promise.

A few letters of sympathy trickled in from relatives as word of her baby's death had spread, and Daisy decided to invite all the clan, including cousins, to a picnic on the farm. Herb encouraged the idea, knowing it would give her something positive to think about.

A Sunday in August was set and all the relatives came for a day of eating and visiting. Planks over sawhorses became tables set up in the flat section of the gently sloping Mississippi River pasture. Everyone brought food with so much left over that the Norton children enjoyed the remains for some days. The only "fly in the ointment" was that Floyd refused to leave his room.

Daisy, ever conscious of her status as stepmother, was chagrined, fearing at least some of the relatives would conclude she had abused him and the boy was thus unhappy. When she complained privately to Herb that evening, he merely shrugged and suggested the boy was like her father-moody.

While Floyd, now a shy thirteen, would never have gone out of his way to make his stepmother look good, he was not consciously trying to make her look bad. He simply detested crowds of people, and having many talkative aunts, uncles, and boisterous cousins swarming around for several hours did not appeal to him. He felt more comfortable in his upstairs room, reading.

"I hate having so many people around," Floyd told Carol preceding the picnic. She, in contrast, looked forward to the times when relatives came, bringing different food, much talk and laughter, and cousins for playmates.

Like most large families, the Norton children did not often seek outside playmates as they had each other for company and plenty of work to keep them occupied. Jean and Carol, however, had found a Protestant family some distance down the county road and occasionally played with Evelyn Bennett.

Offspring of the German Catholic neighboring farmers, most of whom lived beyond walking distance, were not considered a good influence. Especially after Herb caught Ray Behler, from the next farm, showing Floyd how to smoke behind the barn. Ray was sent home with a verbal torrent on the evils of smoking still ringing in his ears. The lecture prevented Floyd from ever taking up the habit, but Ray was unimpressed and, when grown, always smoked when he came to the Norton farm.

Although he did not enjoy the hubbub of family gatherings, Floyd usually entered into the homemade kind of fun his siblings made for themselves. They collected old car tires, which was easy since tires at that time did not last long, and raced them across the rough grassy area in front of the farmhouse which for lack of a better term was called a yard. A lawn with regularly mowed grass, it was not. Herb was too busy to think of running a lawn mower and with five children tumbling over it daily what grass there was never got very high. Daisy had long since ceased to think about how the yard looked. It was all she could do to manage the house and keep the children decently clothed for school.

The southwest corner of the yard was covered with a sprawling woodpile, a convenient shelter for squirrels. Much wood was needed to keep both the kitchen range and the large heating stove in the dining room going from early fall to late spring. A slightly later model than the picturesque potbellied stove of pioneer days, the Norton's stove was an oblong structure with some chrome decor. It was in the centrally located sitting room and provided heat for the entire house except the kitchen, with the warm air flowing up the open stairway, adequately heating the three upstairs bedrooms in all but the very coldest weather.

Late in the spring, when heat was no longer needed, this stove was taken down for the summer, providing welcome extra room. But when the first chill nights of September came, Herb had the annual chore of first resurfacing the stove with shiny "stove black" and then getting the stovepipes fitted into the chimney. The children all had to help keep the wood box full as they grew big enough.

Little Juanita, no longer the cute, plump baby, started school that fall, and with all the children gone, Daisy felt a new burst of freedom. For a few hours on most days she could at least choose her occupation, contrasted to the washing, ironing (with the aptly named "sad" irons which had to be heated and lifted from stove to ironing board), cooking, and cleaning. She spent much of the extra time sewing for the children, often creating an attractive dress for one of the girls from a garment given her by a relative or friend, or even remodeling some of her no-longer-worn teaching wardrobe.

While her seamstress ability helped stretch their few dollars, Herb earned extra income growing corn and peas for a local cannery. The firm, owned by a family named Barr, paid farmers well for a few years. The older children all were pressed into helping pick the sweet corn each fall. They often grumbled about having to arise at unreasonably early hours, but the ears had to be picked before school to arrive fresh at the plant. And they knew that their efforts were helping to provide needed income for them all.

Floyd had graduated from the eighth grade in Soo Falls and followed Daisy's wishes to attend High School in Croquille. Even though it was two miles further for him to walk, she was sure the better course offerings were worth the extra distance. Sometimes the children were given rides by neighbors going to town but mostly they walked to and from school in all but the worst winter weather, when Herb would transport them with team and sled.

Daisy worried about Floyd as he began in the new much larger school in a bigger town; he was so quiet and reserved he made little impression and few friends. She knew it was no use to ask him about it for he would merely shrug. At home he enjoyed the dubious distinction of being the oldest child, which meant his father took special pride in all he did. And like most farmers, Herb hoped his son would become a farmer too.

All four of Herb's brothers had continued in their father's occupation. He and his next older brother, Charlie, had even rented their father's place to start out. But none of his fatherly pride was apparent to Floyd for, like many men, Herb never articulated his love to his sons. He worked hard to support them and thought that was proof enough. And the boys in turn thought of him as a drudge.

He was a hard taskmaster, expecting them to work as long and as hard as he did and was not reluctant to use the strap when he felt the need. Both sons ultimately came to view farming as nothing but unending toil from daylight to dark. They never could take a day, or even a few hours off, to go fishing or for any other pleasure.

Herb, who grew up admiring his hard-working mother and, like her, not appreciating his more jovial father who tended to treat life rather nonchalantly, had known nothing but work. So now, at the height of his family responsibility, he understandably thought of little but keeping ahead of the weeds in the summer and keeping the livestock warm in the winter.

He was especially proud of his older son's ability to handle horses. At an early age, Herb had set the boy astride a horse-no matter that the animal was a workhorse. Having learned to drive a team as a youngster, Floyd was given more responsibility by his father than any of the younger children. This is so frequently the case, that it is no doubt why the eldest child often is more serious and responsible than younger siblings.

"I let him drive the team home with a big load of hay when he was only eight," Herb told Daisy, "and as he turned the corner into the driveway, I just shut my eyes. And he made it all right," he added proudly. But he never mentioned the subject to his son.

8

Neil was hurrying home from school in late March in 1925 when, after crossing the bridge from Soo Falls and climbing the hill to the west river road that led north out of Croquille, he was surprised to meet his father heading home afoot.

Herb, as all farmers of that day, walked many miles in his work but he always drove to town, using team and sleigh in winter. But that day the car had refused to start and a neighbor, who had come over to borrow a shovel, offered to take him to the hospital. Now he was anxious to get home in time for the evening chores, he told his son, wondering why the boy seemed so mystified. It had been obvious at last night's supper that Daisy was gone and he had heard the girls talking about the expected event.

"But why did you go to the hospital? Is someone sick?" the ten-year-old asked anxiously, for he still vividly recalled the trauma of six years earlier, since tragedies are remembered long after routine times are forgotten.

"Your mother-that is, Aunt Daisy, had a baby-a nice little girl," Herb said tenderly, not sure how to refer to his wife as he was aware that Floyd always called her Aunt.

"A baby?" Neil was excited, apparently not having noticed his aunt's growing size nor absorbed the previous night's conversation.

"I wonder what she'll think of Jack," he went on merrily, asking his father if he thought the newcomer would like to ride Babe, the Shetland pony now the children's prized companion.

Herb, listening to the boy rattle on, laughed to himself at the child's lack of understanding about the condition in which babies arrive into the world.

But it never occurred to him to explain this to his son as they hurried home, for Herb's mind was on getting the cows milked on time, lest they produce a few pints less milk. Every drop of cream was needed to take to the creamery as this provided the family's only regular source of income. He already was "stewing," as Daisy affectionately described his frequent discussions about money, weather, or whatever else was bothering him, on how to pay the doctor and hospital bills.

Neither he nor Daisy had talked much about this pregnancy, perhaps afraid that it, too, would end in tragedy. But this time the doctor had ordered her to the hospital a day before delivery where she underwent hot baths. The special attention had paid off, for all went well, to the relief of Daisy's few close friends.

The birth brought no comment from any of the neighbors, for to them Daisy scarcely existed and, since she had hardly attended church during her pregnancy, the momentous event in her life caused little reaction there. All the relatives were glad for Daisy, and Jean and Carol also realized how important it was to their stepmother to have a child of her own.

But Neil was keenly disappointed when the squirming bundle was brought home and, not being told that infants need time to turn into active toddlers, he thought that little Flora, named for her grandmother, was somehow lacking in brains.

To his active mind the word baby, applied to Juanita long after she was tagging after him around the yard, simply meant someone younger than he. The ten-year-old boy, struggling to find his place in the middle of a large family, decided this new baby sister was uninteresting and ignored her for years. Typically, he never discussed his thoughts with anyone. His older brother, to whom he naturally looked for guidance, also ignored her and the boys' lives went on as usual.

This lack of understanding got sibling relations off to an unfortunate start, doubly so because it stemmed simply from lack of communication from an educator to her nephew. The older girls, however, remembering when Juanita was an infant, were not surprised at the baby's helplessness.

Only a mother who has waited till age forty to have a child of her own can know Daisy's newfound joy. She often stood over Flora's crib, gazing fondly into the sweetly sleeping face, thanking God for giving her a healthy child. She vowed to be the best mother possible, realizing in her next thought that she must be careful not to show partiality toward her own child.

She tried hard to be absolutely fair in her treatment of her stepchildren (though she usually thought of them as her nieces and nephews) and was thankful she always had Herb's support.

"You kids mind your mother," Herb would say if any argument arose in his hearing. Daisy tried not to burden him with discipline problems as she knew he was always bone weary by the time he came into the house for supper.

"Why do we have to mind her-she always is yelling," Carol complained to Jean in the privacy of their own room. "Our own Mama didn't yell that much."

Jean, who could not really remember her own mother,

replied with wisdom beyond her years, "She didn't have quite so many children as Daisy," her voice sank to a whisper as she used her aunt's first name. The children were strictly taught to never address adult relatives by first name; use of aunt and uncle became a lifetime habit.

Fortunately, little Flora was a good baby and her routine did not upset the household to any great degree. The annual Coolidge family picnic was especially well-attended that year and all the relatives expressed flattering interest in the baby. Even Floyd decided to participate and kindly taught a younger cousin to ride his bicycle (which his father referred to as a "wheel").

Daisy scarcely left the farm; she had all she could do with the extra washing and inevitable work caused by an infant and she still had not regained all her strength. But force of will and a thankful heart kept her able to keep the house functioning satisfactorily.

That fall, she received news of the death of her father, Berton Sidney Coolidge, on September 9, which was also Herb's birthday. Daisy was ambivalent about her father. He had always been good to her; in fact, as the baby of the large family of eight children, she knew she had been her father's favorite. He would take her with him to sell berries in town. But also she was well aware that he had never been a good provider. A combination of poor health, resulting from his Civil War diet and imprisonment, and his desire to find a milder climate for his health, which seemed like wanderlust, had kept Berton moving his family from state to state before Daisy was born.

She recalled the family story of how they had started out for Texas with their wagon bearing the sign "Texas or Bust." They had busted, her older brothers always recalled bitterly, and had to return to Minnesota to live with relatives until Berton managed to buy a small farm. But after he had gone South, to spend his last years in Heber Springs, Arkansas, where he grew fruit, he never forgot his family and had continued to write long, interesting letters, even a few poems, Daisy thought fondly. He had even written Floyd a detailed letter in answer to his grandson's inquiry about raising peanuts. Now there would be no more letters, she thought sadly, aware of the finiteness of life adults face at the death of their last parent.

But she had no time to brood. Soon Flora was a year old and Daisy scraped together enough extra cash for a roll of film to take the first picture of her darling in her buggy in the yard. That summer, noting how hot the afternoon sun shone into the screened back porch, she enlisted the boys' help to transplant woodbine plants from the woods nearby. She had noted them climbing wild in the woodlot of second growth which was unfarmed atop the hill which, eons ago, she had explained in her best teaching manner, had been the bank of the Mississippi River, now more than a half mile distant. This old bank, some twenty feet high, curved around the edge of the Norton farmhouse yard, barn, and outbuildings, and also provided a sledding site in winter.

The transplanting required carrying pails of water from the well between rains, but within a few years the vines covered the two sides of the porch, providing appreciated shade. Daisy also got the boys to bring in river rocks, eight to ten inches long, easily obtained along the edges of the fields, to mark out the boundary of the front yard. It would keep people, Herb included, from driving car or wagon right up to the door and thus continually wearing down what little grass there was.

That summer Floyd was sixteen and working for a neighboring farmer hauling gravel. Herb, unlike some fathers, allowed his son to keep his earnings for he knew Floyd wanted to attend college. Even though he seemed but a workhorse to his sons, Herb knew the importance of getting an education. Influenced by the Coolidge's bent for schooling, he had attended the University of Minnesota farm school which then ran a program for high school age boys. They lived on the St. Paul campus and experienced college life, albeit learning about agriculture on a high school level. The goal for Herb was to learn how to be a better farmer, but he already strongly suspected that would not be Floyd's aim. His son's college fund also had benefited from the profits from calves Herb had given him to raise over the years.

Daisy had decided to take cake and ice cream over to the gravel pit on Floyd's birthday as it was so late when he got home, the family dinner was long over. She was conscientious in making a cake for each child's birthday, complete with candles, though gifts were sparse and were usually some practical, needed item.

Herb had tried to dissuade her from the undertaking, seeing it as unnecessary extra time and work.

"He won't appreciate it," he told her. "It doesn't matter," Daisy replied with the kind of illogic with which it is hard to argue. "I want to do it for him."

Floyd seemed surprised, but he accepted the cake and by now nearly melted ice cream, with a quiet smile. Herb, suddenly angered with his son for his continuing lack of a show of affection for Daisy, said to him harshly, while Daisy was out of earshot checking on the sleeping Flora, "For heaven's sake, can't you thank her?"

Floyd looked up at him quietly and replied, "Why don't you tell her?" The youth meant no disrespect; it seemed a useless ritual which his dad could as easily perform. But to Herb the words were incomprehensible. More so than some men, he revered women, starting with his mother. He was often hard with his sons, but he would never dream of laying a hand on his girls, and wives were to be cherished.

Fortunately, before he could vent his feelings over Floyd's response, Daisy's voice soothing her little girl who had now awakened, made him realize he could take no disciplinary action in front of her about what he considered Floyd's gross lack of respect.

Daisy, meantime, unaware of her husband's disgust, returned to where Floyd was working, collected the dishes and, after a few brief pleasantries, prepared to leave.

As they were driving home, Herb thought he saw her wipe a tear from the corner of her eye. But when he glanced more carefully at her, she smiled sweetly at him. "I've done the best I could," she thought to herself.

That fall, when a Chautauqua program was announced in Croquille she didn't want to take her toddler out but the Campbells invited the other children to attend with them. They never forgot the excitement of the entertainment provided in the large tent erected across the street from the church.

The Campbells often unwittingly offended Daisy, making her life harder when they meant to be kind. Some years earlier when Neil had been visiting at their house, which seemed so luxurious to the Norton children with its electric lights, plush furniture, and carpeting, Linnie had decided to buy him a pair of long pants, knowing Herb was hard pressed financially.

But Daisy was incensed, not only at the implication that she and Herb could not afford to clothe their children decently, but, more importantly, because she had herself looked forward to buying the boy his first pair of long pants. That was an important milestone in growing up in the 1920s.

9

One of the inevitable results of having no one to neighbor with, or even discuss her problems via telephone, was that during the long hours alone when the children were in school and Herb busy outdoors, Daisy continued to dwell on unpleasant topics.

Women who are employed can always find a minute to discuss a grating personal or family irritation with a colleague but homemakers have to rely either on physical neighbors or telephone friends. Daisy's shyness and inability to make friends easily kept her from developing any meaningful relationships, even with the women whom she met at church.

At times she envied Herb who, while he held definite prejudice about Catholic theology, had no trouble working with his neighbors or doing business with other men in the area, nearly all of whom were Catholic. Sometimes Daisy, succumbing to the typical minority mentality, thought everyone in the county except them was Catholic.

Unlike his wife, Herb never thought much about their social isolation for he saw people regularly in taking his cream to town and conducting his business transactions such as selling livestock or buying feed and hay when needed. Busy as he was, it did not occur to him that the social isolation Daisy experienced was nibbling away at her emotional health.

Even though Daisy was unable, mentally or physically, to inject any variety, let alone adventure, into daily life, sometimes variety comes unasked. One bright fall day a rather disheveled man appeared at the farmhouse, saying he had run away from the Veterans' Hospital in Croquille but now regretted his decision. He appealed to Herb to drive him back "home."

His appearance and manner led Daisy to believe he was suffering shell shock, as so many World War I veterans' psychological problems were described. Herb, as usual unwilling to let anything keep him from milking on time, told the man he'd have to wait until the chores were done. Daisy was uncomfortable having the stranger in the house and suggested he wait in the barn. By skipping supper and milking a little early, Herb was ready to take the veteran back when it was still twilight.

"If I can just get inside the gates before they take the roll at dark, they'll never know I ran away," the veteran told Herb worriedly as they drove the lonely country road leading to the west side of the city where the VA hospital was located.

Herb, reflecting on the coming darkness, suddenly thought perhaps he had been too quick to respond to the man's request. "He could jump me here and there'd be no one to find me for a long time," he thought ruefully. But he kept the man in idle conversation and soon the lights of Croquille assured him no problem would result from his good deed.

Daisy, too, steeped in ideas of service to one's fellow men, had not questioned that Herb should drive him back. It wasn't until supper was over, the children settled to their lessons, and little Flora put to bed that she began to worry.

Floyd and his next older sisters were engaged in a spirited

discussion about some theoretical subject and soon the three of them moved upstairs, the girls voicing indignant scorn for their big brother's ideas.

As the clock neared nine, Daisy felt sure something had happened to Herb and for the first time in her adult life she began to panic.

"If Herb is injured or hurt in an accident and unable to work, what will become of us?" she wailed silently. If he were killed, God forbid, think of the possible legal tangle she would face with her stepchildren, the oldest of whom were now teenagers. The icy realization hit her that no amount of sentimentality over her willing mothering of her nieces and nephews could change the fact she was their stepmother, with all that the term implied. And, listening to Floyd's spirited talk with his sisters earlier that evening made her realize that while he was often silent to the point of rudeness, he had an agile mind and could be very articulate when he felt the need.

Aware that she was letting negative thoughts overwhelm her, Daisy started to turn toward Neil and Juanita who had been studying at the round dining-room table in the sitting room but covertly watching their stepmother, who had been staring out the large window unseeingly into the dark.

"Don't worry, Papa will get home all right," Juanita sidled up to Daisy and put her arm softly about her worried aunt. Daisy, touched by the child's tacit understanding of her worry, hugged the nine-year-old and forced herself to think calmly.

Neil, also sensing the tension and feeling more important with the older three siblings already upstairs, offered the male perspective that his dad could certainly make the trip with no problem since he had just yesterday had the tank filled with gas and the engine checked, practical facts which Daisy welcomed.

Chastising herself, she thought, "Where is my faith? I'm supposed to believe in God's care." But the combination of Juanita's unspoken awareness of her panic and Neil's practical assurance did help. Patting Juanita again tenderly she whispered, "Let's just ask God to take care of him." Years later, in the midst of normal teenage animosity to parents, Juanita always remembered the time when she had offered solace and it had been gratefully received.

Soon the sound of the family car fell on thankful ears and with the two younger children off to bed, Daisy enjoyed a rare chance to talk with her husband alone. He ate the food she had kept warm for him and she heard about his trip which, in retrospect, they agreed had been somewhat foolhardy.

The incident had forcefully made Daisy realize how completely her life depended upon her husband, not only emotionally but financially. If something happened to him, what would happen to her-and Flora? Suppose the children, urged on by greedy lawyers, or even relatives, demanded selling the farm. Daisy was reassured that she could always return to teaching and thus support herself and Flora-after all, she had a lifetime certificate-but she fervently hoped these late night worries would never materialize. During the seven years of her marriage, she had given no thought to her own abandoned teaching career but now remembering that she could always support herself again if she had to soothed her taut nerves.

She had been dimly aware of the changes in American society since her marriage in 1920-that many women had cut their hair, and shortened their skirts. She knew that smoking was now "trendy" among the so-called flappers of the time. But none of this had any real effect on most Midwestern farmwives, Catholic or Protestant, whose lifestyles were long established.

When she was an impressionable teenager attending the little white country church with Myrtie and most of the Norton boys, the pastors had vigorously taught that smoking and drinking, as well as dancing and card playing, were wrong. She even remembered with some embarrassment how a woman member had been "church mauled"; meaning she had been publicly removed from membership because she had worn powder and paint, that is, used cosmetics. Even at the time, Daisy had thought this was carrying pietistic teaching too far.

She and Herb were typical of their generation of White Anglo-Saxon Protestants (WASPS) who firmly believed that foreigners (considered almost synonymous with Catholics) were a source of danger to the English-speaking citizens whose ancestors had immigrated only a few generations earlier. It had become a cultural belief and the little white country church, where the couple had learned well the importance of piety and moral living, had done nothing to counteract the idea.

Although they probably were unaware of its existence, this widespread suspicion of foreigners in the Midwest had spawned the formation in 1887 (when Herb and Daisy were small children) of the American Protective Association in Iowa.

By the 1890s, when they were teenagers, this sacredly anti-Catholic order had spread throughout the Midwest. They may never have heard of the group, which soon gave way to other issues, but the Nortons inherited the prejudice resulting from the heavy immigration in the latter part of the nineteenth century.

Now in the 1920s, most Protestants still felt that somehow their religion and culture must be the most pleasing to God, seeing how the country had thrived under its influence! Ironically, Daisy was long unaware that while she was in church, her older brothers sometimes played cards with their father at home. She knew that both Eva and Bret played bridge and she had no quarrel with what they did. However, since Eva had a hot temper and was known to throw her cards across the room where a niece who helped her reported often finding them behind the stove, Daisy felt that one could make a sin out of any activity by acting like that. It did not upset her when both Floyd and Carol learned to play bridge at Bret's home after they were in school in the Twin Cities.

The founders of Methodism, John and Charles Wesley, had frowned upon card playing, Daisy knew, because in eighteenth century England it was associated with gambling for high stakes and drinking in taverns. Playing a friendly game at home was entirely different, she realized, but it was just not part of either her or Herb's life.

Likewise, passage of the Eighteenth Amendment, bringing Prohibition, meant nothing to Daisy. People should know more than to waste their money and harm their health with alcohol, she firmly believed. And while she noted that ministers at the city Methodist church were not as strident in discouraging use of alcohol as when she was a girl, for her such moral issues had long been settled.

She would have been horrified had she known the effect upon Floyd's retentive mind when he overheard a conversation between his dad and Uncle Jim Campbell concerning Christian ethics.

The Campbells frequently visited the Nortons though Daisy avoided their house as much as possible. One Sunday night as Herb was milking, Jim came to the barn to ask his advice about a vexing problem. He was under business pressure to deliver bread on the Sabbath and even though, as a staunch official board member of the Croquille Methodist Church, he knew this was wrong, it seemed necessary to keep his business prospering.

What did Herb think? Herb, ever practical and really not caring what his brother-in-law did, agreed that doing business on Sunday was wrong, but if it had to be done, he shrugged . . . How about getting drivers who didn't attend church anyway to make the runs? Unknown to either of the men, their casual discussion of whether to apply Christian ethics to everyday living had shattered Floyd's youthful idealism.

Listening to the talk while feeding the horses, the boy decided "If that's all Christianity means to them, I don't want any part of it," and silently vowed to have no more to do with a church occupied by hypocrites.

Had he discussed the matter with Daisy she could have eloquently quoted him scripture about not judging others and, more importantly, explained that one's own faith never depends upon another person's conduct. But, even if she had said them, her ideas would have been like the good seed planted on rocky soil which soon withers under the harsh sun. Floyd had learned the Ten Commandments by heart at his mother's knee and so they had become sacred words; to have the two most important males in his life disregard them was to him proof of how fickle religion was. How vast the void between learning about God and having His love permeate one's heart!

Daisy, in contrast, while sure of her Christian faith, knew life still has to be lived on a daily basis, and she increasingly found herself unable to keep her home as well run as she would like, producing constant frustration and guilt. The never-ending cooking, cleaning, and washing and ironing left her little time or energy to promote any cultural activities or even give any individual attention to the children. But she urged them to read and, with the books she had brought from

St. Paul added to the library of her late sister, the Norton children did not grow up ignorant of the classics and music. She and Myrtice had each owned a glass front bookcase. Now the two, each six shelves high, sat proudly on either side of the three windows in the parlor which looked beyond the wraparound front porch to the Mississippi River pasture and its landmark three elm trees. Visiting neighbor children were impressed with the many books.

The Nortons also had an Edison phonograph and on Sunday afternoons when they could relax, the children sometimes played the thick records. One, a humorous verbal dissertation on the Fourth of July, always brought peals of laughter from the childish listeners.

Curiously, despite her lifetime interest in church and attempts to attend whenever she felt able, Daisy sometimes used Sunday afternoon, when a late dinner gave her relief from one evening meal preparation, to clean furiously. This was never planned but it happened often enough that Jean, for one, decided this was her aunt's way of getting even with the Lord for the hard life she led.

There was no philosophical reason behind Daisy's seeming inconsistency. She often did not feel energetic and had to push herself to keep going, so when a day came that she felt up to extra work, and especially if Herb was napping as he usually did Sunday afternoons, and the children were busy with their own activities, she seized the few uninterrupted hours to clean. Having the rooms clean and neat lifted her spirits.

Sunday was the one day Herb did no farm work except for the necessary care of the livestock. Even when hot winds threatened to lodge the ripening grain and he paced the parlor and sitting room floors "stewing," nothing would ever have induced him to work on Sunday. But he paid little attention to his wife's housework routine.

One Sunday while Daisy was vigorously mopping the linoleum-covered floors in kitchen and sitting rooms, Carol came in from outside to tell her that Jean's finger was swollen and she was worried about it. The girl had run a sliver into it several days earlier, but said nothing, and now the finger had become infected.

Daisy knew that such a simple hurt could become serious if not attended to, and she was wildly casting about in her mind how to attend to it and still get her allotted cleaning done before evening would bring the family back into the house expecting at least a light supper. Suddenly she had a solution to both problems.

"Tell her to go over to Behlers and have Mrs. Behler put a poultice on it," she instructed Carol. The Behler house was visible across the field and up the road and since the German families butchered regularly Daisy knew Mrs. Behler would have salt pork to use for a poultice to draw out the sliver. So Jean dutifully trudged over to the neighboring house alone and the kindly Mrs. Behler did as Daisy had requested.

When the children came in for popcorn and apples, the living area of the farmhouse was shining and in a few days, the poultice had done its work.

10

In 1928, when Flora was three, Floyd, whom she called "Woydie" as she was unable to pronounce his name properly, graduated from high school. The entire family attended the commencement exercises, one of the few times they all went anyplace together. It was a new experience for Flora who had scarcely left the farm, except for the few times Daisy had taken her to church with her. The child responded by crying in fear at the first large crowd she had ever seen.

That summer Daisy's brother, Robbie, who had long lived out West, returned to Minnesota for a visit. A former schoolteacher, he now worked for the Bureau of Reclamation in Montana. His wife had died a few years after their marriage, leaving him with one cherished daughter, also named Flora, who was close in age to Jean and Carol.

The three girls had fun together and the visit occasioned a Coolidge family gathering at the Norton farm, at which even Aunt Eva seemed in good humor. When the inevitable snapshots were taken, with the extended family gathered by the large stock tank and well located at the edge of the lawn, Neil had the dog Jack standing on his hind feet while little Flora, at ease within the family, beamed happily.

Juanita, barefoot, posed saucily bending over with hands extended on her knees. Other pictures taken during Robbie's visit caused Daisy to wince, for one showed the outdoor privy clearly visible through open barn doors, even though the object of the snapshot was Robbie and his youngest niece.

In many ways this brother, the only one of Daisy's siblings to leave Minnesota, was different from his brothers. His one child contrasted starkly with the large families of the others. Perhaps for this reason, he seemed to have more money. While not rich, Robbie was generous, even-tempered, and the few dollars he spent on extras such as ice cream endeared him to all the Nortons. And since he did not farm, but supervised delivery of water in a faraway state, Herb had no reason to criticize him.

That Christmas he sent Daisy three dollars for her little Flora and the teddy bear bought with the money was the only stuffed animal the child ever had. Without any playmates her own age, she often amused herself by creating a series of imaginary companions, to whom she gave silly names.

When Floyd left for college that fall, Daisy was rather shocked to find how little dent it made in the household activity, although with one less "hand" to divide the farm chores, Neil had more to do. Not surprisingly, he easily absorbed the extra work, showing more interest in farm activity than his older brother ever had. It almost seemed as though more, not less, was accomplished. There were no more disruptions such as the one last summer when the boys had gotten into a violent argument over their regular task of carrying the milk can into the house. Each one wanted to use his right hand, twisting their steps to try to accomplish this. When Herb, hearing the ruckus, looked out they were partway up the hillside with the milk can swaying precariously between them. Now, with no one to argue with, Neil seemed as much help as the two boys had been together. And when his dad arranged for the boy to ride one Saturday with Joe Trout, a farmer who had begun trucking cattle to South St. Paul, Neil was elated.

Herb and Daisy were proud that by careful saving they were able to augment what Floyd had earned from his own livestock so that their oldest son could attend his mother's (and his aunt's) alma mater, Graylin University in St. Paul. Daisy gladly offered to do his laundry, each week getting a carton of dirty clothes in the mail and returning them clean and pressed although often her cervical bones ached from standing over the ironing board.

Soon a new domestic problem erupted. Carol and Jean, who had generally been dutiful and helpful daughters with the unending housework, now rebelled about the long-legged underwear their parents insisted they wear to high school, because they walked the three miles each way.

The girls had pointed out, in vain, to Daisy that they were so hot in class they perspired, as the Croquille High School where they had followed Floyd, was well-heated. Herb, particularly, was sure if they did not wear the underwear they would catch cold when they walked.

"We're much more likely to catch cold going outside wet with perspiration," Carol retorted. And, adding insult to injury, Daisy also made them wear black cotton stockings (the city girls had light tan ones), because she insisted they would not show the dirt so readily. The girls promised to wash them daily and after much discussion, the battle for both stockings and underwear was won by the girls, with the strict provision that if they caught cold, the underwear would return. Even after they were grown, the girls often wondered why Daisy, with her teaching experience, did not realize how the black stockings made the Norton girls embarrassingly conspicuous.

That fall, Herbert Hoover was elected president, much to Herb's relief, for he admired the man whose name he shared and, like most Protestants, he believed Al Smith's election would have endangered the nation. A Democrat was bad enough, but to have a Catholic in the White House would be unspeakable.

Midwest farmers had yet felt little impact from the deteriorating economic conditions throughout the country which were to climax in the stock market crash the next year. The only local indication of trouble was the failure of the cannery to pay farmers for their corn and peas that year. Herb worried over the situation while Daisy and the girls kept reassuring him the payments would be made eventually. Their hope was in vain as the firm soon folded.

As long as enough rain fell to grow the grain, hay, and corn which provided livestock feed and some cash income, farmers lived, if not well at least without worry of hunger or loss of their farms into which they had poured so much sweat and toil.

In 1929, now known as the start of the Great Depression, Daisy was able to purchase a new Maytag washer, with its gasoline-operated engine. It was a great improvement over the previous wooden washer whose agitator was hand-operated, even though water still had to be carried in and heated on boilers on the stove, and the wringer was still hand-operated. She and Herb were thankful they could pay cash for the machine and they believed the new president's campaign promise of better times ahead.

Another major improvement was the installation of a chemical toilet in the basement. It was simply a large pail lowered into a metal frame with a covered seat housed in a small closet.

It had to be carried out and emptied when full, but it meant no more cold trips to the outdoor privy or emptying chamber pots which everyone used winters and in bad weather.

Daisy breathed a grateful sigh when Herb tore down the old eyesore. Now, if we could only have running water and a bathtub, she thought, knowing full well the cost was out of the question.

As often happens, just when life seems to be moving satisfactorily, trouble comes uninvited. Herb's purebred Percheron brood mare whom Daisy had named Thoa, became ill. Herb knew she was going to die; he had again heard a loon call just as he had ten years previously, heralding his first wife's death. Since Daisy shared his love of horses, the impending disaster posed not only an economic loss but an emotional one as well.

So Herb practically ordered Daisy to go visit Eva, thinking it would spare her witnessing the depressing details of disposal of a dead but beloved horse. Appreciating his concern for her, Daisy dutifully packed, including a few paper dolls for little Flora so she could play quietly, and drove the fifty miles to her sister's house.

Even though she knew Herb had meant the visit to spare her, Daisy returned home after a few days more depressed than if she had never left. Being in her sister's modern home, with the long-lost but not forgotten luxury of a bathtub, had only sharpened Daisy's despair of ever again having the modern conveniences she had left when she came to the farm.

As usual, Eva provided no comfort, pointing out that she herself had only obtained a nice home after leaving the farm. Daisy smarted at the implied criticism of Herb, when Eva noted that they could move into town because of her Billy's skills in carpentry as well as in farming. "I can't imagine Herb doing anything but farm," she continued rather scornfully. Daisy, angered at her tone, rushed to defend her husband but there was no denying who had the modern house-plus the bathtub.

This time the loon's ominous call produced the feared result. Thoa was gone, along with the potential income from sale of her foals.

The next year Carol finished high school and opted to enroll in nurses' training at Asbury Hospital, a church-related teaching hospital in Minneapolis. She had been a caregiver since her earliest years, willingly helping, as oldest daughters have long been expected to do, with younger siblings. She had even made doll clothes for Juanita, whom she always considered her special charge.

In 1931, Jean graduated as salutatorian of her class, the only one of the family to achieve this honor, although all were good students. By this time money was getting even scarcer as farm prices were now reflecting the spreading shock waves of the growing world economic downturn.

Since going away to college was financially impossible, Jean uncomplainingly settled for attending Teachers' College in Croquille and was thankful when her Aunt Linnie offered her room and board in exchange for help with the housework.

That same fall little Flora started first grade, walking the mile and a half to Soo Falls in company with Juanita, by now a self-conscious eighth grader. Although the younger girl was much lacking in social skills, having spent nearly all of her life by herself, she sensed her sister did not want to be seen with her during the noon hours. So she dutifully mixed with her own classmates during the hour-long lunch periods when children could use the playground equipment or even roam on the wooded hillside behind the school.

Compared to today's first graders, she was ill-equipped to

begin school, having never associated with children her own age nor scarcely held a pencil. She was not at a disadvantage, however, since most first graders then started with no previous structured learning experience, and they all learned quickly the rudiments of socialization now provided in pre-school and kindergarten.

Because she had been read to and surrounded by books, Flora found learning to read pleasant and even though she experienced some cultural shock in leaving her placid, isolated existence, she did well in school. But she was always glad when Friday afternoon came, and as she grew older this became sort of a byword between Flora and her dad.

Juanita graduated from eighth grade in the spring, sharing joint valedictorian honors at the Russell Grade School. Daisy pinched the few dollars which came in from the daily cream check to purchase material to make her a graduation dress. With three of the children now gone from home, she thought finances should ease a little but she saw no improvement. When she discussed this with Herb, he assured her it was not poor management on her part; prices of everything sold from the farm had gone down and were continuing to decrease.

It was 1932 and President Hoover's unwillingness to intervene in the mounting Depression plus his now bitterly resented prediction of improvement was already haunting the Republicans. Breadlines were forming in the cities and farmers unable to eke out mortgage payments, nationwide were losing their farms.

Herb, whose farm was mortgaged to the previous owner, a German named Schmidt, had been unable to pay on the principal some months, but he always had kept up the interest payments. Now he was frantically worried that he would be unable to do even that.

Daisy, knowing his desperation, determined to swallow her pride and ask her sister for fifty dollars to tide them over till harvest. Without telling Herb her reason, she drove down to her sister's home one Saturday when Juanita could stay with Flora. She never would have stooped to ask for herself, but she hated to see the worry in Herb's eyes and his restless sleep. So intense was her concern for her husband she scarcely had given a thought to how the request would appear to her sister.

So she was both shocked and hurt when Eva sharply turned her down, without even considering any alternative.

"They have the money," Daisy thought angrily. "If I had any money and a brother or sister was desperate, I wouldn't even worry about when or if they could pay me back."

Eva insinuated that the Nortons would lose their farm anyway, so why send "good money after bad," the old ill-timed saying grating on Daisy's nerves. But with her usual self-containment, she didn't let her sister know how deeply she was hurt and upon her return home, told no one of her humiliating rejection.

That fall voters elected Franklin D. Roosevelt, already tagged as FDR by headline writers. Even though the Nortons had loyally voted for Hoover, they had been somewhat impressed by his "nothing to fear but fear itself" inaugural speech. But like all Republicans they saw his expansion of federal spending as a threat to the American way of life, even though it benefited them a little.

The flurry of FDR programs aimed at turning the economy around and, more importantly, creating a climate of hope, allowed Jean to get work at the Teachers' College. There she heard that a woman was wanted to teach sewing reconstruction evenings at the high school. When she told Daisy about the opening, her aunt immediately applied and got the job. The class was for women to bring in old coats or any type of clothing and, with the teacher's help, learn how to remodel the garment into something wearable. Daisy was confident there was no kind of reconstruction she could not handle.

She hated leaving Flora each evening, but the child was safe, if lonely, with Neil and Juanita both home and Herb milking in the barn.

The sewing class only lasted through the winter, but Daisy earned enough money for a much needed adult bed for Flora who was still sleeping in her old crib, from which the end boards had been removed.

As spring came with its yearly promise of good crops, a couple named Clock appeared at the Norton farm, expressed an interest in buying the place and appeared eager to look it over. Herb did not want to sell the farm where he had worked so hard for the past fifteen years, even cutting trees and breaking several acres to enlarge the back fields. He wanted to keep paying on the place and stay there until all the children were through school.

But he and the real estate agent dutifully walked the couple over much of the farmland and pasture. The Clocks said they ran a restaurant in town called Clock's Tick-Tock Cafe, a play on their name the woman pointed out, causing Herb to think she considered him too dull to recognize their cleverness.

Somehow their interest in the farm didn't ring true to Herb, but after several visits from them, a crisis over the mortgage caused him to forget everything else.

Mr. Schmidt appeared pompously at the farm one day, informing Herb he would foreclose since Herb was behind in his payments. It was a scene repeated with sickening frequency across the land.

There was even a juvenile version for, as their fathers talked, the Schmidt son went with Neil to inspect his rabbits in the little building on the hillside which the Schmidts had used for a smokehouse.

"This really is our place, not yours," the boy loftily told Neil.

11

In adversity remember to keep an even mind.
— *Horace*

Daisy shared Herb's panic when he reported what Schmidt had said, but through long habit and reflective of her New England heritage, she managed to keep outwardly composed.

"We'll find some way out," she told Herb, thinking immediately that if she could go back to teaching there would be some steady income. But she knew women teachers forfeited their careers when they married. If only she could somehow be back in St. Paul and still be here too, she thought idly.

While she mulled the impossibility of her teaching and remaining on the farm to mother the children, Herb's mind was busy on another track.

"I'll tell him he never gave me a clear title to this farm," he told Daisy, ignoring the obvious fact that since Schmidt held the mortgage, the title could not be clear. Daisy, seeing Herb's growing excitement, refrained from pointing this out.

"I'll tell that so-and-so that if he forecloses, I'll sue him for every penny I've paid him since I bought the place," Herb cried, gathering enthusiasm for his proposed argument as he talked. "Germans are always scared when you mention the law, because they are all so ignorant," he continued. Daisy knew that no ethnic group had a corner on ignorance, but she had to agree with Herb's appraisal of the mostly second-generation German-American farmers in that area. Mention of a lawyer would make him hesitate to take any legal action, she hoped.

Meantime, she had read in the newspaper about the Federal Land Bank as an agency available to help beleaguered farmers. When she mentioned this to Herb, he was doubtful about whether he could qualify and so the matter rested for several weeks.

Life was at a low ebb for Daisy. The constant worry about finances plus lack of medical attention had taken a toll on her health. In addition, years of not seeing a dentist for lack of cash to pay for it had resulted in a mouthful of rotten teeth. When the pain became more than she could stand, she finally went to a dentist who informed her all he could do was give her gas and take them out.

She would have to go to the hospital to be given the anesthetic. How they would ever pay for this she didn't want to think about. But Herb said it had to be done; she couldn't go on this way.

When she came home from the morning hospital stay with only six bottom teeth, still feeling woozy from the anesthetic, she was at least cheered to learn that Herb's bluff had worked on the harried Mr. Schmidt.

"I scared the daylights out of him when I threatened to sue him," Herb told his wife. But while the confrontation, which Herb later enjoyed retelling many times to his children, gave them a breathing spell, it did nothing to provide the necessary money for payments.

However, as often happens, adversity brings intangible benefits. Their hard times had brought Daisy and Herb closer together. In their ability to discuss their problems, she no longer felt any stab of jealousy if occasionally Myrtice's name arose; in fact, they both sometimes enjoyed laughing about her.

Herb had recounted how the first year he and Myrtice had lived on the present farm he came in one night from milking to find her, the hired girl, and the older girls seeing how high they could kick on the kitchen door!

And recently he had told Daisy in great detail how in a vain effort to teach his first wife promptness, he had driven to town without her, after sternly warning her he would do so if she weren't ready at a set time.

"He loved her when she was his wife, but he loves me now because I'm here and she's gone," Daisy thought, thankful Herb was practical, as well as sentimental, but not one to brood over the past.

When she went to her room to rest after the dental surgery, she was pleased and comforted to find a note on her pillow in Herb's rough handwriting. It read:

"In your heart my love has found a home where it shall always live."

It was addressed to "My Darling Daisy Ada" and signed "Your boy, Herbert O. Norton" with several of the words boyishly underlined.

Daisy was still in poor health and worried over how they would make ends meet, but she sank into bed with a lighter heart. If only she had energy to make something special for Herb, like the lemon pie he so liked! Then she thought, that's the wonderful part of real love: one doesn't have to always DO something. Bonded in their mutual affection, they could face the bleak economic future with more confidence. As soon as Daisy felt able, she quietly talked to a bank official in the little hometown bank in Soo Falls, and learned the address of the nearest Federal Land Bank: St. Paul.

While worry over money and health problems induced by lack of medical care seemed to overwhelm Daisy, she found some comfort in her faith. But the Protestant churches of that time seemingly were wrestling with their own problems of belief. While the rethinking of the once taken-for-granted literal interpretation of Biblical stories was happening on the highest church bureaucratic levels, at least in the Methodist Episcopal Church, it had the appearance of heresy to some in the pews.

Herb and Daisy, nurtured in their most impressionable years in the pietistic Bible-centered theology of a little country church, did not appreciate the onslaught of higher criticism. Daisy, secure in her own personal faith and more open to intellectual controversy than her husband, let most of the questioning of long accepted precepts "go in one ear and out the other" as she laughingly said. But for Herb it was different. He had faithfully attended a men's Bible class Sunday mornings at the Croquille church, even when Daisy, secretly ashamed of her one worn Sunday dress, stayed home.

One Sunday he came home furious over the discussion in the class. Some of the men had openly questioned the story of Moses leading the Israelites through the Red Sea.

"They said there was no way the waters could have parted like that," Herb stormed. "They laughed at the idea God could do it. What do they know about it, anyway," he continued; a question many times repeated by disgruntled church members, no longer sure of what to believe.

Daisy urged him not to be upset by what a few local men said; after all the Christian church had gone on for centuries despite many differing beliefs. But her lofty mental stance failed to quiet Herb's indignation and he never attended the class again-nor church services, except a few times when his youngest child was involved in a program.

Nonetheless, he continued to drive Juanita and little Flora to Sunday School. Supported first by Myrtice and now by Daisy, he had faithfully seen that all the children attended Sunday School. But as each got into high school they, like youths for centuries, lost interest.

The financial worries of their parents, while superficially known to the teen-aged Neil and Juanita, made no impression at all on Flora. She was blissfully unaware that the wide open fields and pastures where she liked to wander might no longer be home and her older siblings, preoccupied like all youths in planning their own futures, paid little attention to their parents' worries.

All of Daisy's stepchildren were much aware of how she favored her own child, but since she tried to be fair in her dealings with them and the older ones had left home while Flora was still small, there were few overt problems. Juanita and Neil, who had more years to observe the favored child, mainly put it out of their minds and had each other to confide in when they had complaints.

Fortunately Flora was a fairly quiet child, but she was not above childish thoughtlessness and was the recipient of a few retaliatory tricks from her brothers. Once when Floyd was home from college and she was playing in the haymow, he shut the large door which when laid flat shut off the stairway to the first floor of the barn. A larger child could have lifted up the door, but Flora could not.

However, her dad soon realized what had happened and opened the door, berating his son for ungratefulness when Daisy was uncomplainingly doing his laundry and mailing him clean and ironed clothes.

Another time Neil, tired of the little girl bothering him, locked her in the corncrib, a building some distance from the house, placed conveniently close to the hog house. It was made of laths with open space between each row. A sharper child would have known she had only to reach a hand through the open space between the laths and turn the wooden knob. She did not realize this, and soon someone came by and let her out before she could become panic-stricken.

Whether or not she was aware that her mother's overwhelming love was generating dislike from her siblings, the child avoided confrontation, and basking in the assurance of that love and her protected, quiet life, kept much to herself. She never told her mother of the two minor incidents.

But that summer she became the not-so-innocent reason for a harsh showdown between Neil and his stepmother. The child had been thoughtlessly throwing corn off the top of the rabbit hutch on the side hill where Neil was drying it for his rabbits. He warned her several times to leave the corn alone and when she continued upsetting his work, he struck her.

Flora ran crying to her mother, as any small girl would, even though she was not seriously hurt. Unfortunately, to Daisy whose nerves were already taut from the heat and unrelenting housework, it sounded as if her darling had been injured and she tore out of the house to confront the offender.

"What did you do to my child?" she screamed, dimly realizing she was over-reacting, as Flora, who was following her, obviously was unharmed.

"I told her not to touch the corn I'm trying to dry for my rabbits," the boy told her. "I've worked hard on this and they're my rabbits. I won't have her ruining my work. I've told her if she touches one more ear, I'll spank her," Neil went on with dignity.

Daisy knew he worked hard to care for the rabbits and the child undoubtedly was in the wrong. She might have calmed down had not Flora, unmoved by the furor she was causing, grabbed another ear with the predicted result. Daisy, reacting blindly, rushed to stop Neil's action and the boy instinctively shoved her back.

A more agile woman could perhaps have withstood the push and not lose her footing. But Daisy, who had never regained her slender figure after her first child, was large and not in good condition. So she fell and rolled down the rest of the gentle hillside across the rough wagon road leading to the upper field, and onto the yard.

Carol, home for vacation from nurses' training and viewing the fight from the kitchen window, thought Daisy would never quit rolling. Neil was scared when he saw what had occurred but, too full of righteous indignation at being blamed unfairly, did not much care if she were hurt. "If Dad beats me for this, I'll run away," he decided. "I'm in the right and I won't take it from her anymore."

Daisy awkwardly got to her feet, limped back into the house, and went to bed. Whether or not she complained to Herb, the children never knew and, such was her reserve, they would never have dreamt of asking. The incident was never again mentioned among them nor did Herb say anything to Neil about it.

And Flora, with the exasperating blithesomeness of childhood, already had forgotten the trouble she had caused.

12

The lack of money and resulting increasingly rundown appearance of the family farmhouse and barn was more painful to Juanita than any other of the children. Now an insecure teenager, she poured out her unhappiness by writing a private journal. Because of her interest in writing she became friends with a popular classmate who often invited her to her home. But Juanita, embarrassed over the worn rug and old car, always had some excuse as to why she could not reciprocate.

She dutifully learned household skills and particularly liked to iron early in the morning, before either Flora or her mother were up. Juanita enjoyed the peaceful atmosphere of the big kitchen at that time of day, her mind free to imagine while she ironed, her father's periodic entrance with the fresh milk bringing her a cheerful touch of reality. Herb always was kind to his daughters, especially Juanita, left motherless as a toddler and the youngest for seven years. When she was smaller and cried or was unhappy, he would let her hold a small china dog he owned and this always seemed to comfort her.

Herb often thought fondly of how he had chosen her name. Myrtice had been reading aloud to him, a practice he was happy to have Daisy continue. The heroine in the western novel had been named Juanita and he had told Myrtice, "If the baby is a girl, let's name her Juanita." Her middle name, Ellen, was for Grandpa Coolidge's maiden sister.

Daisy, who found it hard to fall asleep at night in the often stifling house, cooled only by sporadic and often warm night breezes, had taken to sleeping till mid-morning, a habit inherited, Herb felt disapprovingly, from her father. She had a hard row to hoe, as the old farm saying goes, and she worked hard whenever she was able, so he said nothing.

Despite her poor health and growing mental depression resulting from social and physical isolation from all but family, Daisy was more acutely aware of the emotional problems of her stepchildren than was their father. She realized Juanita's deep feelings of insecurity, even though she was a bright girl. Daisy's teacher friend, Blanch Atkins, had asked permission to give all the Norton children IQ tests as part of a research project. She had been very professional, never telling any of them the results, but Daisy knew her youngest niece had ranked the highest, something at which her brother Neil would have scoffed had he known.

Neil, she felt, while bright enough, was over-confident and cocky, often belittling Juanita in their youthful discussions. Life will knock that out of him, she told Herb. Lack of self-confidence is more serious, she knew, and she often worried silently about how she could help the girl gain more self assurance.

She sometimes secretly wondered if the fact that Juanita had been kidnapped when an infant, although only for a matter of minutes, had contributed to her feeling of inadequacy. Myrtice had once confided to Daisy, on condition that she never tell Herb, that the summer Juanita was a baby she had taken the children to the county fair. While Herb and Floyd were involved with the animals they were showing, Myrtice briefly took Neil and his two older sisters to look at a few exhibits, leaving Juanita asleep in the back seat of the car. When they returned only a few minutes later, Myrtie had been horrified to find her baby gone.

Fortunately, her worry was short-lived, for a man standing nearby, noticing her concern, immediately informed her that a woman had just taken the baby and he had thought something was wrong. Now, feeling vindicated for his suspicion as well as important in his helpful role, he eagerly volunteered to lead the distraught mother to the would-be abductor in the grandstand. The baby soon was back in her mother's arms, but for reasons any mother can understand, Myrtice never told her husband about the incident. It resulted from an innocent enough impulse, which many mothers of large families have followed, often from necessity, to leave a sleeping child briefly unattended, but it could have ended tragically.

Myrtie, her sister thought fondly, had the knack of coming through improbable events unscathed. She remembered the time her sister, in her often unthinking merry way, had gone to town with unmatched shoes. When someone mentioned it, she had only laughed gaily; Daisy would have been mortified had she ever been so careless.

Herb, being of a practical nature, paid little attention to his wife's psychological comments about the children. His basic philosophy was the Lord helps those who help themselves and he tended to like people who worked hard and criticize those he considered lazy, giving little thought to the nuances of personality quirks.

He was always up at sunrise, hurrying through the milking

and feeding of livestock to put in long hours in the field during the spring, summer, and fall. Work, he often said with sometimes grim satisfaction, was the only thing he knew. His father, he thought bitterly, never had put in the long hours he did. From the time Herb and his older brothers were old enough to handle a pitchfork they had assumed most of the farm work. His father, a heavy, jovial man, would come home from town, jump off his wagon, toss the reins to his sons, and order them to take care of the horses, while he strolled into the house demanding supper from his hard-working wife.

"If I did that, the horses probably wouldn't get fed or rubbed down," Herb would mutter to himself. But despite their father's cavalier attitude about work, Herb and his four brothers all grew up to be farmers. Now, he noticed, not only Floyd, but his nephews were leaving the farm as soon as they finished high school, as were youths throughout the Midwest.

The boys realized what their fathers tried to ignore: that no matter how hard they worked keeping weeds down and rotating crops to help replenish the soil, if no rain fell the effort seemed useless.

However, despite endless worry and fretting, so far the corn always had matured to provide silage and some grain was harvested, both to use as feed and for a cash crop.

Daisy was becoming increasingly bitter about the hopelessness of farming in the Midwest. She knew how hard Herb worked; the only advantage for him, she often thought ruefully, was that he fell asleep the moment his head hit the pillow, eliminating any opportunity for her to have any private conversation.

There has to be a better way to make a living, she thought, almost daily. One moonlight night, when Herb decided to cut grain by its light, she told Flora bitterly, "Whatever you do, don't marry a farmer." The child, surprised by the shrill tone of her voice, wondered silently about her mother's remark, for she loved the farm.

The never-ending work routine was broken only on Sunday or when relatives came. The Coolidge picnics had stopped as Daisy's siblings were even more strapped for cash than the Nortons, especially her brother Gene, who seldom had money to buy gas for his old Buick.

For several summers, Herb and Daisy went to Gene and Lucy's home for the Fourth of July. With only Juanita and Flora to take, as Neil by now declined to accompany his parents, traveling some forty miles was no longer such an undertaking. Her brother's eight children all were still at home, even though half were through school. Herb privately thought them a shiftless bunch, but there was no denying the warmth and camaraderie in the large family. They always seemed happy despite their lack of worldly goods and the Norton girls, despite their age differences, each looked forward to the trips, as there were congenial cousins for both.

Like many childhood events, the yearly July Fourth visits ended too soon for the girls. Gene died in 1934 and on July 4, the Nortons were embarrassed to have the sweet-faced widow, Lucy, and her girls present them with a gift for Neil who had graduated from high school that spring. It was only an inexpensive necktie, but Herb scolded en route home, pointing out that the family should never have wasted their scarce dollars for even the least gift, ignoring the obvious fact it was something they wanted to do.

Daisy, too weary to argue, said nothing. She had dearly loved this kind older brother and the nieces and nephews with whom she had spent so much time before her marriage. She was thankful that, so far, her three oldest children were getting some education beyond high school, something she could see Gene's children would never have. But she also observed, somewhat wistfully, their lack of money had not made them act or think in the pinched, limiting way she was beginning to. Neither did it seem to affect their happy outlook on life, as she knew it was doing to her, and apparently to Herb as well, to hear him rave about the innocent necktie.

Determined to change the subject, she pointed out the wildflowers along the road.

"See the black-eyed Susans!" she cried.

"Oh, you mean the brown-eyed Daisies," Herb fondly replied, and the girls in the back seat realized this was a private joke between their parents, symbolizing their growing affection despite the harsh circumstances of their lives. Whether they knew which was the correct name-or if either was-didn't matter. It was a special bond between them.

However, Daisy's insistence upon calling the common roadside flowers another name was more than good-natured joking with her husband. It stemmed from her deeply felt dislike of her own name, which did not fit her, she knew. The name brought to mind some flea-brained, happy-go-lucky girl, not the reserved, serious person she was. How many countless people go through life with names they dislike?

When they got home, Neil took the nicely wrapped gift without comment and no one ever knew whether or not he appreciated the sacrificial gift as he was becoming increasingly distant from his parents. He had a job at the Great Northern roundhouse and was saving his money so he could go to Chicago and attend a technical school where he could learn about radios.

Daisies Don't Tell

Despite the lack of electricity, he already had brought the magic of a radio to the farmhouse by using a battery he charged from the gasoline engine used to operate the pump. At first he had only earphones, but soon he got a cabinet model and the novelty of world news, Amos and Andy, and the Ford Sunday Hour brought a new dimension to Daisy's isolated life.

One evening that summer, the Nortons were surprised to have a car drive into the farmyard containing Daisy's "city brother" Bret, and Eva's fun-loving husband, Will Pepin. Bret had driven up from the Twin Cities that evening, picking up Will at Elk Grove about halfway, a remarkable feat to the Nortons, who considered going down to Minneapolis or St. Paul from their farm an all day's drive.

But there was an urgent reason for the surprise visit. The men informed Daisy that her brother Sid had been put in the insane asylum after a violet confrontation with his long-suffering wife. Actually, officers had put him in custody after his wife and children had fled, frightened for their lives, in the middle of the night.

Daisy, who had gone out to the car when she saw them getting out, as if fearing bad news, was embarrassed. She knew of her father's violent temper which Sid had inherited and she understood how his constant battle with poverty and drought could drive him to the breaking point.

But what would Herb and the children think, she wondered confusedly. Bret and his brother-in-law were all business. They intended to pull strings and get him out of the institution which, because of its stark name, struck fear of mental illness deep into the public's consciousness. Bret's position as a respected teacher in St. Paul gave him contacts which would be useful, he assured his worried younger sister.

Daisy was relieved to hear their plans and secretly pleased they would make the long drive to confer with her. But, she thought sadly, she, Eva, and Bret were the only family left, and Eva apparently was letting her husband handle the problem. Robbie, out West, need never know, Daisy thought gratefully.

Her deeply felt pride of family caused her to downplay the situation and when Herb finished milking and they all sat in the kitchen, she allowed Flora a few minutes of silliness showing her uncles how she could let a ball go from the top of her one-piece summer playsuit and roll down inside to come out at her knees. She steered the conversation to farming before leaving to put her child to bed and when the men left, the bleak impact of Sid's insanity, temporary or not, had been somewhat lessened by general talk.

At least the older children need never know, she thought thankfully, and was especially glad Juanita was spending that night with a friend. Flora was too young to understand.

Bret's efforts were successful; Sid was soon released and spent the rest of his years alone on his farm with his two boys. Anna divorced him and took their four daughters with her to Minneapolis, where they lost all track of Sid's family.

13

Heaven arms with love those he would not see destroyed.
— *Laotse*

The rainfall had been spotty and a major worry for several years but by 1934, the Dust Bowl was in full force in the states south of Minnesota, where the open prairie, its native vegetation long ripped away by the plows of eager farmers, was now showing its resentment of human tampering. Dried by relentless wind and no longer held together by the long-rooted prairie grass, the top soil was blowing across the eastern United States, and a little blew north as far as central Minnesota.

One spring Saturday, it suddenly became dark by four o'clock. Daisy hurriedly called to Flora who was out playing on rocks behind the shed. In wet years, the rocks were in the midst of a little runoff stream which drained from the sheep pasture into the ditch along the county road in front of the farm buildings. But now it was just a deserted area cut off from sight by the machine shed. To a solitary child with imagination, it represented adventure and Flora went in to the house reluctantly.

The kerosene lamps had to be lit long before it should have been dark and the dust seeped in through all the window frames, leaving small waves of dirt on the unrailed wraparound front porch where the children had played when little and where Daisy sometimes dragged her rocking chair to catch any fleeting evening breeze.

But while discouraging and slightly frightening, the dust storm had lost its fury by the time it reached Minnesota, and the disturbing darkness only came once. However, residents had little energy to pity their counterparts in Kansas and Nebraska who were enduring the dust-filled darkness day after day-and abandoning their farms.

The next day, Daisy secretly got out an old letter from her desk, certifying her lifetime teaching certification. She would apply for a school in the Twin Cities-or anywhere there was a vacancy-take Flora, and leave Herb and the two teenagers who could manage through the week, she thought wildly.

Knowing full well that Herb would never approve of such a move, no matter how helpful her paycheck would be, she determined to say nothing to him until it was all settled. She recalled, ruefully, that her first real fight with her husband had been to convince him that while he was allowing Floyd to raise calves and keep the money for college, he should also allot lambs or something comparable for Jean and Carol. It had taken much effort on her part and Herb had been "peeved" with her, but Daisy's innate sense of fairness demanded that girls be treated equally with sons. Actually, the money from the lambs which Herb had "donated" under protest, was used to purchase doll buggies for the girls, but Daisy always felt justified in that initial fight.

This battle to earn money for their mortgage payments, buy her badly needed false teeth, let alone a few new clothes for

Juanita (the list went on and on) might even be more difficult, with Herb's stubborn English male ego.

To keep the peace as long as possible, Daisy broke all habit and walked the mile to Soo Falls to mail her application. Her stepchildren later laughed to think Daisy, who never walked anywhere, had hiked the two miles without Herb knowing about it.

Juanita, who was a perceptive teenager, wondered why her mother seemed somehow in better spirits, despite her lack of decent clothes and teeth. The girl was secretly embarrassed about her mother's empty mouth and she avoided ever telling her when parents were invited to high school events.

Daisy watched for the mail eagerly; she knew there would be no avoiding a confrontation with her husband when it came.

"But we need the money so desperately," she thought. "It's not as if I were going to use it for myself." She dreamed of being able to have Juanita attend college, with maybe a decent Sunday dress for herself again, forgetting momentarily that to teach she would have to be dressed presentably for the classroom.

When the eagerly awaited envelope came, Daisy snatched it before Herb's wondering eyes and hurried into their downstairs bedroom. He heard her cry out in strangled tones and rushed in, thinking she must be ill.

Daisy was sitting on the edge of their bed, staring unbelievingly at the paper in her hand.

"They won't take me! I can't teach! My certificate has expired!" she repeated over and over. "I can't ever teach again without taking more classes and there's no money for that."

She looked up at Herb beseechingly, eyes brimming with tears. "I had so wanted to earn some money to help us out," she said in a dull voice.

Herb, gradually realizing the length to which she had gone

to seek what she assumed would be a job for the asking-an obvious admission of his failure to support his family-first felt angry and hurt at his own inadequacy. But, sensing her utter despair and realizing that all her effort had come to naught, he refrained from saying the bitter thoughts of every husband when faced with the grim reality that he is no longer able to support his family.

"Well, it's too bad," he said, not with complete honesty, "but don't worry, we'll get by somehow. I always have." Herb looked out at the parched lawn and fleetingly admired his wife's guts.

Always self-employed, he never had been forced to risk the humiliation of such a turndown. His only work outside the farm was for such minor jobs as putting up snowfence or hauling gravel for the county for road construction. Later, mulling the episode over in his mind while milking, he had to face the uncomfortable possibility that Daisy, had she obtained a job, could easily have left him for good.

Since it was a moot question and, afraid to hear her answer, he never asked her point-blank what she had planned. Any woman with any brains would be smart to get out of this kind of life, he thought bitterly.

The idea of a woman teaching, gainfully employed away from home during the week and returning only on weekends, was unheard of. What would his German neighbors think? Suddenly, with the deep sense of propriety which both helps and hinders middle-class people, he was thankful they need never know.

They avoided the subject and none of the children were aware of the devastating letter. Juanita dimly realized that something extra was depressing her mother, but with the normal self-absorption of youth, she gave it little thought.

Daisies Don't Tell

Sunday afternoon, after the usual lull in farm work for Herb, when Juanita came downstairs after writing her private thoughts in her journal, she realized Daisy was nowhere around. Flora was playing with paper dolls in her room and Neil had gone to work at Campbell's bakery, where he earned extra money on weekends.

When Herb awoke from his nap, he went out to the barn to feed and milk the cows as he did every night of the year. Still tired from his nap and used to having Daisy busy in any part of the large two-story house, her absence made no impression on him. But as he brought in the first can of fresh milk and saw Juanita's wondering face, an icy fear crept over him.

What had she done? Had Daisy been so dejected about her turndown and so depressed over their financial hardship that she'd do something violent to herself? But what could she do, he thought with practical instinct. She couldn't hold a gun. The Norton men never had been hunters and the only gun in the house was an old .22 rifle Neil had gotten to kill crows.

What could she do, he thought distractedly. Drown herself? They had gone swimming a few times in their first year of marriage when both were young and had energy; it seemed a century ago now.

But how could she even accomplish drowning as low as both rivers were? The practical kept emerging in his wild thoughts. And furthermore, she would never kill herself and leave her child he reasoned, to halt his panic.

But looking at Flora, who was silently watching him, apparently by now aware of her mother's unexplained absence, Herb decided he had to do something. So he phoned the bakery and asked his brother-in-law, Jim, to let Neil come home. Even though he hated to have to admit the reason for such an unusual request, he felt it only fair to explain.

"Oh dear, oh dear," Jim repeated in a worried tone. Herb, who had no great love for his brother-in-law, whom he suspected of somewhat too cunning business deals on occasion, felt the man's sincerity. The bakery owner had recently got into legal trouble under the National Industrial Recovery Act, one of the few New Deal agencies designed to soften business opposition. He apparently had violated some provision and Daisy had privately laughed about his predicament, unaware her stocky, genial relative had often defended her when his women folk assailed her first as too "citified" and now as unfriendly. They found much to criticize in their poor relation on the farm, who had no decent clothes, but who despite her obvious poverty still, to them, seemed uppity.

Soon Herb's brother, Charlie, who had never married and lived with the Campbells and also worked at the bakery, arrived with Neil, who was excited, first at the novelty of being brought home unexpectedly by his uncle, and then dimly wondering what his stepmother had done to so alarm his father.

He noticed his uncle's grim face as they drove the three miles from town in the early dusk and remembered the gossip he had heard that Charlie had once been interested in Daisy who, secretly in love with Herb even when he was courting her sister, had quietly deflected his interest.

As is common for youth, Neil found it hard to see how anyone could have been attracted to Daisy who was now heavy, with sallow complexion, a prominent nose, and her hair still done up in an old-fashioned knot on top of her head, which failed to soften her lined face.

When they reached the farmyard, Neil was wondering if

Jack, their beloved shepherd dog, now grown to maturity, would be any good tracking. But where could she have gone in the rough fields and steep river banks in the pastures? She'd never be able to climb any of them, he thought scornfully, yet realistically, aware of Daisy's poor physical condition.

Charlie, feeling for once in his lonely life an opportunity to even temporarily take charge of his usually more competent younger brother, urged phoning the sheriff's office at once. While Herb mulled the wisdom of admitting his wife was perhaps unstable but possibly had fallen and was lying injured, the men asked Juanita to light the lamp so they could look up the phone number. Flora, standing dumbly in the kitchen, was directly in front of where her sister needed to walk.

Usually Juanita would have curtly ordered her little sister out of her way, as siblings routinely treat the younger ones. But this time there was such a difference in her tone as she asked Flora to please move that the young child instinctively thought, "They think Mama is dead. That's why she's talking so nice to me."

The sheriff's office was called, but before any officer was dispatched to the rural home, a shadowy figure slipped around the corner of the house. The men were back out in the yard talking in worried low tones, when Charlie looked up to see Daisy go into the house.

Silently, the three men separated, Herb to finish his chores and Charlie and Neil to return to the bakery. None said anything about the cancelled search; it was a topic all wanted to forget.

Flora asked her mother where she had been, and when Daisy told her she had just gone for a walk, and put her to bed and heard her prayers as usual, the evening's trauma evaporated for the little girl with childlike ease.

Juanita, vaguely sensing her mother's upset mental condition, pointedly did not mention the absence, reminding herself that for a woman used to hiking, Daisy's walk and late return would have been routine.

That's what I'll say if anyone ever hears about it and asks, she thought, like her dad, wanting to cover up any indication of mental instability.

But in her heart she knew the walk had not been routine.

14

Daisy pretended that she was asleep when Herb came to bed, thus avoiding a confrontation over her unexplained disappearance. She would simply tell him-and anyone else who dared ask-that she had to get away by herself, she thought determinedly.

But her mind still raced with one after another of vivid scenes, flashing like a motion picture across the screen: of walking blindly through a long cornfield...of somehow being on the bank of the Mississippi...wondering what it would be like to let the still strong current overcome her hot, weary body.

Where was God in this? Was He watching over her in her fight to find courage to keep going when all seemed hopeless? The scenes came and went in her mind until even she did not know for sure just what had happened, or where she had wandered.

But she had one stark, disruptive memory which, mercifully, eventually crowded out all other worries. Sitting at last to rest under a spreading oak tree on a neighboring property because it opened on a small picturesque lake, Daisy had been rudely brought back to reality by the unwelcome appearance of Fritz Behler, whose land adjoined the Norton farm on the west.

Herb, whether in jest or irritation, had often privately accused Fritz of deliberately sowing Canadian thistle seed on their property, and this was the first thought that crossed her mind when she realized he was leering at her, or thus it seemed to her turbulent mind.

And when the elderly man said, in what she perceived as a simpering tone, "Are you meeting someone here?" Daisy, realizing with horror and disgust how he would enjoy telling the neighborhood she was having an affair, went completely wild.

"Get out of here and leave me alone," she screamed, startling the farmer who, despite Daisy's prejudiced mind, had merely asked the question for something to say.

"Can't I ever be alone?" she yelled. "You don't know what it's like being the only Protestant in a whole country of god-damned German Catholics!" causing the startled farmer to wonder briefly if she wished to convert.

Once unleashed, the years of pent-up frustration and loneliness came tumbling out into the uncomprehending ears of the simple farmer. "It's just not being poor-I know no one has much money-but the endless work, never seeing anyone but critical in-laws and damned German Catholics who can work but have no education. I never see anyone who has even heard of Wordsworth or a sonnet." At this point, she glared at Fritz so that he shifted uncomfortably, vainly wishing he had turned away when he spotted her.

"You don't know what it's like raising another woman's children," she shrieked, losing all control and thinking that at least she would make him realize she was not cavorting with another man.

"And now, just when I thought I could do something to help out, I find even the damned life certification is invalid." She stopped, thoroughly confusing the elderly farmer, who also was just out for a Sunday walk, albeit a less agitated one.

He drew back, aware that she was totally upset and figuring the sooner he left the better. While none of the German neighbors had much money either, they did own their farms and so did not face losing them. He dimly recalled she was Herb's second wife and he supposed being a stepmother was harder than raising one's own children. As Daisy talked on and on, her voice often breaking into a near sob, he thought of the only time he had seen his kindly, timid wife nearly this upset. It had been when their younger son, Andy, had accidentally shot a companion in the arm while hunting. The boy, very likable and extremely good-natured, had been drinking and the injured youth's parents, also German Catholics notwithstanding, had threatened to sue. Fritz had cooled the situation with some of his hard-earned money.

His older, more responsible son, Ray, was now farming the home place. But the two boys were all he had wanted to handle and Behler realized the distraught woman ranting before him was trying to raise six.

As he tried to think of something to say, Daisy again yelled, "Just go on; leave me alone!" which he hastily did.

Now, lying rigid in bed, Daisy was horrified to recall her emotional outburst. Would he tell Herb how she had sworn at him? What would Herb say or think? It would be her word against Fritz, who conceivably might not react kindly to a neighbor woman yelling at him.

Herb will just have to choose between believing me or that damned German, she thought. Like all reserved people, she was devastated to think how she had disclosed all her problems to this man, basically a stranger, although he had eaten in her kitchen many times.

As she finally dozed with exhaustion just before dawn, her last thought was that she hoped she had so confused him with her wild ranting that he would never mention the unfortunate encounter to anyone.

And apparently Daisy was correct in analyzing her effect on Fritz for, to her knowledge, he never brought up the subject and was extremely respectful of her at the next threshing crew supper at the Norton home.

15

Daily routine has the effect of not only dulling joyous times, but also covering over unhappy or embarrassing ones, and thus life continued as always in the farmhouse. The only outside mention of Daisy's disappearance was a brief note in the weekly paper, put in by Herb's sister, Linnie, a kindly, simple woman who could never conceive of the emotional turmoil in her sister-in-law's mind. Taking the incident at face value, she had given the information for the personal column items so popular in that day, saying merely that Mrs. Herb Norton had become briefly lost Sunday night.

Daisy, scornfully reading the item, said that was just like Linnie-not knowing enough to mind her own business. The children, who all had benefited from their aunt's kindness, had learned not to respond to such statements and no more was said.

Soon there were more positive things to think about. Jean, who had completed two years at Teachers' College, thanks to being able to board and room with the Campbells and earn a little money in the New Deal program to hire students, was planning to marry.

Herb and Daisy were much against the marriage for while

the boy, Steve Rankin, was pleasant enough, he was a little younger than Jean, a mere 19, and worse to the strait-laced Nortons, they felt his father was of questionable integrity.

He had been in many types of businesses, sometimes rich, sometimes poor, and Herb was convinced he was not always ethical.

"He's so crooked he can't lie in bed straight," Daisy repeatedly said, using the old expression so seriously that Flora, ignorant of verbal hyperbole, often wondered how the man whom she had never seen, could sleep.

The most obvious reason the couple should not marry, her parents emphatically said, was that neither Jean nor her boyfriend had any job, money, or house. Herb, thinking back to his first marriage, stormed that he had a farm bought with a house waiting when Myrtice and he were married. Jean listened patiently, but went on with her simple plans. She had met Steve at the church and wanted to be married there.

Meantime, Carol, now a registered nurse and working at the hospital where she had trained, was keeping company with a young man from a family the Nortons respected. John Baldwin was the son of a distant cousin of Daisy's and he worked in his parents' lumber business. The contrast between the two courtships was considerable.

Juanita thought it most romantic that Jean was buying silverware in the dime store where she worked, getting basic items at the very cheapest price. But Carol, scorning such a niggardly existence, was thankful that her fiancé came from a family of substance. She was determined to have nice things when she married, and since she was now earning a modest salary, she was able to start out with a much more impressive household.

To Flora, however, the little sister who was always in the

way, the two future brothers-in-law were a contrast of a different sort. While John politely ignored her, Steve who was majoring in education, taught her how to identify elm, maple, and oak trees and took an interest in her childish ideas.

The drought that summer had dried the grass in the sheep pasture, so named because it was mostly used for these animals, and as the land did not border on either of the rivers, its only source of water, the frog pond, had long since dried up.

So Herb was forced to find somewhere else to put his farm flock of some thirty head of sheep. A cousin, Ray Norton, was a trucker and Herb got him to truck the sheep to the northern part of the state where pasture still existed. Herb and his good-natured cousin, whom Flora teasingly called Ray Coon, a name she had learned from the Burgess Animal Book, left with the sheep two days before Jean's wedding.

"If I don't get back in time for the wedding, don't leave till I get here," Herb told his daughter. The young couple, in company with Steve's parents and younger siblings, were starting out west immediately after the ceremony. Steve's father had decided there was still opportunity to make one's fortune out West.

"We won't even have the ceremony till you do get back," Jean told her dad with feeling. Flora, hearing the conversation, was relieved to know her dad was that concerned about Jean, for there had been much criticism of the upcoming wedding.

But Herb got home in time and the only hitch—other than the newlywed's lack of money—in the wedding was that the old Norton car had a flat tire, making the bride late to the church.

Part of the family had been driven to church earlier so as to not crowd Jean's organdy formal, a dress she already had purchased for a college function. When Neil started into town with

Daisy and the bride, a tire blew just as they were going up a small hill, ironically by the Catholic church, which served as a cathedral.

It was within fifteen minutes of the time for the service and Jean longed to walk rapidly, as she had done during the years she and Carol had hiked the three miles each way to high school. But, knowing how difficult it was for her mother (she had always considered Daisy as her mother) in the heat, she stifled her impatience and they finally arrived at the church, just as her cousin, Alta Campbell, in her take-charge manner, was coming down the stairway to find out what was holding up the action.

"Let's get this show on the road," she told Jean emphatically in the tone used in talking to domestic help, which Jean had been in a sense in the Campbell house.

Alta's dominating manner had increased with her years, especially since she was a teacher and had recently been named a school principal. Daisy burned with mingled shame that their car was old and not dependable, but even more with dislike for Alta's patronizing airs.

"Why couldn't she just sit in her seat and keep quiet?" she thought angrily as she settled wearily into her own seat. Since it was, of necessity, a small wedding, the ceremony was held in the church parlor. Afterward, the families of the newlyweds stood outside and socialized briefly. The Campbells and Jean's two friends, who were her bridesmaid and soloist, were the only other guests. None of her sisters was involved in the small wedding party.

Afterward Jean remarked that it would have been nice if the Campbells would have seen fit to provide a cake-not too difficult with their bakery-but they made no offer. As neither the young couple nor the bride's parents had money to provide anything, there were no refreshments. After the event was duly captured by camera shots on the church lawn and Herb sternly told his new son-in-law to take care of his girl, the Rankins started on their long journey and the Nortons and Campbells went wearily home.

The next day was Sunday and Daisy was glad to rest while Herb napped. She no longer cleaned house on Sunday as Juanita did most of the major cleaning now. When Herb awoke they settled in the sitting room where she resumed her reading aloud of Zane Grey's Desert Gold.

While lack of adequate rainfall continued to be a major worry for central Minnesota farmers, fate-or perhaps providence-now offered a way to keep the Nortons from losing their place. After Herb's strong verbal attack on Mr. Schmidt, the Nortons were able to transfer the mortgage to the Federal Land Bank. They benefited, like many other beleaguered farmers, by the foreclosure moratorium declared by the New Deal to halt the loss of farms.

Then a man employed in Croquille, T. Charley Buchanan, came to the farm one day, seeking to buy an acre of the Mississippi pasture on which to build a home. He and his fiancé both worked in town but after they married they wished to build a new house in the country. Although unrecognized at the time, these years saw the beginning of a major shift in living patterns which within decades would alter the American landscape forever.

Since the Rural Electrification Agency lines were now installed on the county road, new residents or old could have all the conveniences of the city, provided they could pay for the hookup, and still keep the quiet rural setting with its wide view of the Mississippi and the wooded pastures.

A price of $100 per acre was agreed on and the Nortons

gratefully applied it on their mortgage, but soon learned that officials at the Federal Land Bank took a dim view of the sale. Having farmers sell off small parcels of their farms was a new idea and the bureaucracy in St. Paul was unwilling to break tradition and give clear title to just one acre.

Herb stewed, called the St. Paul officials uncomplimentary names, and racked his brain for ideas. Then he recognized one of the top signatures on the formal, intractable letterhead as a former classmate at the University of Minnesota Farm School.

"You write that so-and-so and remind him I used to help him out when we both lived in Albright Hall," he told Daisy, "and he'd better come around and release that land. After all, they have all the money for it."

Daisy's letter put the information in more tactful words, but the association with the Class of 1908 seemed to soften the official, for eventually the title was provided. T. Charley, who never had any doubts he would obtain it, had already started building his new home, hiring Herb to dig the basement with team and scraper.

Soon the idea of building homes in the country spread and a small shopkeeper in Croquille bought several acres on the steep bank of the Soo River pasture across the road from Buchanan's lot. The lower part of the pasture had never been much used as even the cows avoided the steep bank where the river turned southward after flowing quietly along a flat, low area. As the river turned the corner, it was flanked by a twenty-foot high bank on the side of the Norton property. Atop the bank this section between the small tributary and the Mississippi formed a narrow neck of land before the rivers merged. Few people driving the curving country road were even aware they were on a peninsula and after the road crossed the bridge over the smaller stream the land widened out like a middle-aged spread.

The Norton children, in earlier years while briefly selling milk to the Johnsons, the only family living in this narrow section, had sometimes picked their way along the bottom of the steep bank. A large, forbidding rock protruded from the top of the bank, causing whichever child was delivering the milk to scurry hurriedly past the spot. Daisy had always worried about the rock after they mentioned it to her, but she was fascinated by the various formations of the river bank, having grown up along the Mississippi near Elk Grove.

The new owner, Olaf Gustafson, who operated a shoe shop, looked upon his new land purchase with different vision than the former owners. He wanted the new house built on the edge of the hill where the bank sloped down to the bottomland and, by pushing out the dirt excavated from the basement, he secured an area large enough for a gentle driveway down into his basement garage.

After hiring Herb to dig the basement, his plans gradually took shape though he, his wife, and their adopted son, Buddy, first lived in a simple one-room cabin hastily built on the lower land along the edge of the small Soo River. Buddy, several years younger than Flora, provided a welcome playmate, as she had never been associated with anyone younger than herself.

Since his mother, Madeline, apparently had been unable to have children of her own, Flora sensed how cherished Buddy was by her. As he got older he occasionally came to the Norton farm and would listen to Flora, who by now could play simple popular music on her mother's piano. There was no money for lessons, but as her mother could help her and, mostly because no one forced her and Flora had to find things to entertain herself, the girl became fairly adept at playing from her mother's old sheet music. Buddy always asked her to play one piece in particular—"Good Night Sweetheart"—hardly appropriate for two pre-adolescent children thrown together only by the happenstance of being neighbors.

Once when Buddy was there and Daisy was working in her oft-neglected flower beds, the boy, looking carefully at her, said with the deadly honesty of childhood, "You're an old, old woman, aren't you?" Daisy, realizing that without teeth she looked much older than her fifty years, smilingly agreed.

16

That summer a continued lack of rain plagued the area and one of the German farmers who lived some miles "inland" as Herb always referred to the farming country away from river and railroad, agreed to drive into the Cathedral in Croquille daily to pray for rain.

Daisy, sitting on the front porch to cool herself, noticed his car go by day after day, and both she and Herb were impressed by the man's faith. It didn't eliminate the drought, but a brief rain did fall and somehow crops managed to mature.

While the Protestant couple had to admire the faith of their Catholic neighbor, they were conversely irritated by the insistence of a sister-in-law, Alta Norton, that they must have got rain because it had rained further south where she lived.

"We got rain; you must have got it too," she would declare in no uncertain tone to Herb, who seemed unable to convince her that whatever the reason, no rain had fallen on his farm.

Perhaps it was because of the merging of the two rivers, although the little Soo tributary to the Mississippi seemed too small to have any effect on anything. In the spring, the river was high enough to provide water for cattle in the pasture. But as the dog days approached in August the level was too low to reach under the fence which Herb had built a few feet out into the rivers in both pastures to keep the livestock from bothering his new "city" neighbors.

When school opened in the fall, officials in Soo Falls where all the Norton children had attended grade school decided to start charging tuition for children who lived outside the district. The river was the boundary line, but it had never been observed. Now a growing area of homes (impolitely called "Shanty Town" by untactful neighbors) being built back from the main county road a mile from the Nortons was bringing enough children in from the west side of the river to cause concern, so the tuition was charged.

Daisy, aghast at having to pay money for a child to attend public school, transferred Flora to the grade school on the most northern end of Croquille. This added another mile for the child to walk and she found it a little upsetting to go into a new school, but the classes were smaller and Daisy was pleased to see a reading area in the rear of the room.

Meantime, plans were progressing for Carol's wedding to her distant cousin John. Daisy worked feverishly to have the house spotless as Carol had decided on having a home wedding. She was pleased that Carol wanted to hold the ceremony there and as the bride-to-be had money for essentials and to hire a woman to help with the serving, it need not have been an overwhelming task for Daisy.

But her inborn perfectionism, plus her always constant awareness of the shabbiness of the old farmhouse, as usual wore her down. She made new dresses for Juanita and Flora as well as the bride's dress and soothed Carol's worries that Uncle Fred, who much enjoyed long, loud, argumentative discussions, would be disruptive.

John's only sister, Nancy, a kindly, unmarried woman with whom Daisy felt comfortable, arrived early the day of the wedding and, seeing several unfinished projects, quietly began to help. Three sofa pillows Daisy had wanted to recover were lying unfinished, so Nancy soon had them neatly hemmed. When the guests arrived, the open stairway spindles had been intertwined with autumn leaves and once again a bride marched down the worn stairs and across the sitting room to the parlor windows overlooking the Mississippi River pasture with its three elms, which Daisy now fondly referred to as "her" elms.

Carol had arranged for an arch, also covered with autumn leaves, before which the young couple took their vows. The father of one of Carol's best friends, a pastor, officiated and all the relatives enjoyed the chance to see each other again and visit. This time they did not have to commiserate about the economic status of the newlyweds.

Floyd, who had been working at Yellowstone National Park to earn money to continue college, arrived in time for the ceremony, adding the special glamour of a young, attractive, bachelor brother. Daisy was delighted to see him and tried hard to refrain from plying him with questions. She so wanted to know how things really were with him. The West had become a mystical place to her and Herb, who avidly listened to the Zane Grey novels she read aloud to him. The legendary life the popular author portrayed served as a badly needed respite to the farm-bound couple.

Was it really different from the Midwest? She had only been out of Minnesota once, to Atlantic City on a tour as a young woman, and had become ill, partly because she had worn herself out helping handle luggage for herself and for Blanch, her crippled friend, in the excessive heat.

Did Floyd now feel he could complete his college? How did he like the West? But she never learned the answers, for she knew from his first reply that he did not welcome real communication. As he had from childhood, Floyd kept his thoughts to himself.

As Carol's friends from Minneapolis left, after expressing appreciation for the lovely wedding, Daisy was weary but satisfied. She had always felt inferior to John's mother, Elizabeth, a distant cousin whom she had known since childhood. Elizabeth's natural self-confidence, bolstered by marriage to a well-to-do husband and life in a large town house, had given Carol's mother-in-law a regal graciousness which always made Daisy feel inadequate, no matter that her pride kept her outwardly composed.

Flora, who had wanted to stay up late for some of the leftover wedding cake and ice cream, had fallen asleep on her bed, with the kerosene lamp still burning. Tenderly, Daisy helped undress the sleepy child and tucked her in, thankful that she still had many years before Flora, too, could leave home and marry.

Daisy, aware that her daughter, already backward socially from her isolation on the farm, would have trouble making friends at her new school, urged Flora to invite her classmates out to the farm, a few at a time.

The child was amazed to find that for her city-bred friends, coming out to her farm home and wandering the pastures along the rivers seemed exciting. Once, when the girls removed their shoes to wade in the shallow Soo River, one guest carelessly put one shoe too near the water where it was swept away in the current. The child, Sylvia Benson, hurried back to the farmhouse and, fearing parental displeasure, appealed to Daisy to help her find it.

Herb, working in a nearby field, wondered when he saw his wife accompanying the girls who were now going a second time down the road to the pasture, but she signaled there was no human crisis. Alas, the shoe was never found. Flora, though, was now invited to some of the girls' homes for lunch and her place in the small class was thus assured.

Juanita, meantime, struggling with her overwhelming lack of self-confidence, could only note with some bitterness the effort her stepmother was making for her own child. However, she also was honest enough to realize that Daisy could never have helped her in the same way, for Juanita, more aware of economic status, was embarrassed over lack of electricity and indoor plumbing, which seemingly had no effect on her younger sibling.

At Halloween, Daisy, who was in a period of better health with resulting energy, planned a party for five of Flora's classmates. She designed the invitations, picked up the children, supervised games, served their meal, and returned them to the school at the time noted on the cat-shaped, orange construction paper invitations.

Flora had no more part in the arrangements than if she had been a guest. It was not until years later that she realized her mother might have done her a bigger favor if she had let her help in the planning.

She did feel guilty, however, while she and her friends were being served in style in the dining room, realizing her dad and sister were eating alone in the kitchen.

The next year, Neil left home for Chicago where he enrolled in Coyne Electrical School, to learn about radios, which by now had brought the world to the ears of farm families. The Nortons had benefited from his interest for several years with the battery-operated radio he maintained for them, and Daisy had been thrilled the first Christmas Eve when they heard at 6 p.m. on the farm, Big Ben chimes in London striking midnight.

Now Neil was gone, leaving a void in the shrinking family, for even though in his last years he had often withdrawn from family activity, the boy was basically gregarious. Daisy worried about his lack of sophistication going into a large city.

"There are women," she told her uncomprehending small daughter, "who prey on innocent farm boys to get money from them."

Flora saw Neil's absence as a chance to escape always having to wipe dishes for her sister, by offering to help her dad outside. Juanita, being seven years older, understandably felt she should wash and her little sister wipe. Daisy agreed it would be more peaceful without the girls' daily arguments and Herb was pleasantly surprised that a girl would want to help with farm chores. As long as his two sons were home, the ancient division of work between sexes had been unquestioned.

After having endured Floyd's diminished interest in farming as he grew older, and Neil's recent lack of communication, Herb was grateful to have his youngest eager to help. Every night after school, Flora would climb up the enclosed ladder on the silo, pitch down silage, and carry it by bucketfuls into the barn for the cows. He soon got her a new bushel basket, learning as most parents do, too late for their oldest children, to encourage any positive interest.

For the first time in her ten years, Flora felt important and needed and she rather enjoyed telling her schoolmates she had to hurry home so she could help with the chores. When a friend, not understanding what the word chores meant, repeated

Flora's comment but said she had to get home to "fix the chores," the family had a good laugh.

The drought was broken locally in 1935 and the Nortons had a fair crop. Daisy's spirits revived, especially since she was at last able to get new false teeth. Because she had gone so long without replacements, she had difficulty adjusting to the new teeth, but she bore the discomfort in stoic silence.

At the urging of her "schoolmarm" friend, Blanch, she started teaching a class of sixth grade boys at the Methodist Church in Croquille, but she soon realized the preparation she demanded of herself was more than she could do adequately. Also, the church school leaders expected teachers to attend monthly staff meetings which required driving back into town at night.

The church was experiencing the uproar which strikes every denomination periodically when the pastor is unpopular. In this case, the criticism was mostly pointed at the minister's wife, who, as Herb's other sister Retta reported scornfully, would "often go home from a church meeting with a sick headache." This was believed to be only an excuse to not fulfill her duties as a pastor's wife.

Daisy felt more at ease with Retta, although she was sharper-tongued than Linnie by far. Retta, a widow on limited income, also lived in Croquille but on a much more modest scale than her sister. She rented her upstairs bedrooms to teachers, as many genteel widows did. Although Retta had lived a respectable life with her second husband, Daisy knew she was the black sheep of the Norton tribe, having had a "shotgun wedding" years earlier with the brother of Linnie's husband.

The reluctant bridegroom had soon disappeared. Retta returned with her child, Laura, to her parents' home, caring for them until their death, when her siblings gave her the parental home. Her brother-in-law, Jim, a solid citizen and a pillar of the church, had always been particularly kind to Laura, undoubtedly ashamed of his brother's unfaithfulness.

The fatherless girl had spent many happy hours at Jim and Linnie's house, playing with her cousins. Laura had benefited from much attention from her uncles, some of whom, including Herb, had still been living at home when she was small, and grew up happily, but with some learning disability. She was nearly flunked at the local Teachers' College by Daisy's friend, Blanch. When she mentioned the problem of Herb's niece to her as one teacher to another, Daisy for once forgot her reserve and vigorously urged Blanch to be lenient; she knew that Laura was competent, but slow, and needed to get her teaching certificate.

Daisy would never have dreamed of mentioning her intervention but somehow, knowledge of Retta's unhappy early life softened the chip she carried for most of her in-laws. Now Laura, who had become a successful teacher, was married and living in Montana. She wanted her mother to come live with her. When she left for the West, Retta gave Daisy her large potted fern on a huge stand, perhaps an unspoken thank-you.

But before she left, there was much bad feeling in the church to which they all belonged. The Depression was in full swing, people were short of money to buy necessities, so not surprisingly, the church's finances suffered. And, while Reverend Nelson did his best, he was unable to refrain from often scolding his congregation, which in turn only provoked more negative reaction.

The worst outrage occurred when, for reasons known only to God and the finance committee, the Nortons, along with all church members, received in the mail a list showing amounts donated by each member. Herb and Daisy were outraged, as were many others. Eventually their cries were heard by conference leaders and a new pastor was assigned.

Dr. Harlan Spencer was blessed not only with a kindly manner but a sweet wife. He became a shining example of Christianity to Flora, planting the seeds of lifelong church loyalty, and a comfort to Daisy, calling on her several times in her periods of depression. Herb, although he seldom attended church, had no complaint about him.

Poverty has many facets. It is one thing to not have money to buy something special, another entirely to go hungry. Thanks to their home grown potatoes, milk cows, and chickens, the Nortons never went hungry, although their diet was often monotonous.

But a subtler aspect of poverty is what it does to naturally generous individuals when they no longer can give to charity. As a devoted Christian Daisy understood one should share one's material resources, simply because that is what God commands.

She had always given generously to the church in whatever town she was teaching and so felt upset that they could not now give on any regular basis. Herb's disgust with the lack of belief in the Bible of the Men's Sunday School class had not really affected their willingness to give.

Churches were not the only institutions suffering because of the Great Depression. Daisy's alma mater, Graylin University, like all church-related colleges, also was going through a financial crisis. Some loyal professors, already wearing threadbare suits, had gone for months without salary.

When a man came to the farm to request financial help for the beleaguered college, he refused to accept Daisy's assurance that she would gladly give if she could, but there was simply no cash. They had no checking or savings account. Purchases were made only from the two dollar to three dollar daily income which depended on the amount of cream taken to the creamery that day. When the well-intentioned college agent kept insisting that she must give something (the poor man had received nothing but turndowns all day), Daisy's nerves shattered and she yelled, "There's an old dead hog out around the hill, take that if you want," and slammed the screen door.

The startled man hurried back to his car, muttering that people all seemed to be losing their minds-perhaps because of the heat!

17

While the Great Depression and drought are generally considered to have run throughout most of the 1930s, the year 1936 will long be remembered for the wild buffeting Mother Nature inflicted on the Midwest. In January, the temperature dipped to forty degrees below zero. Flora probably enjoyed the paralyzing cold more than anyone, welcoming the days her mother decided it was too cold for her to walk to school. Since she was a good student, her frequent absences seemed to have no effect on her grades.

On January 22, the morning that residents awoke to the record-setting forty below, the water tank in the barn froze over solid, despite the fact the cow barn was full to capacity with twelve now-shivering animals. Herb spent most of the day carrying hot water from the house to thaw out the tank. It was too cold to think of turning the Holsteins out into the barnyard, and cleaning the gutters, getting in bedding and feed kept Herb going all day, assisted briefly by his youngest daughter. When she complained of cold feet while bringing in straw, he sent her back to the house.

Daisy, meantime, kept putting wood and coal into the

two stoves in the house which seemed to burn fuel faster than she could stuff it in them. The bitter wind blew cold in around the windows and the inside of the kitchen door was covered with hoar frost. It never had been this cold in St. Paul, Daisy thought dejectedly.

When Valentine's Day came, Flora suddenly wanted to go to school. She started walking, but luckily got a ride about halfway. Daisy had taught all the girls never to accept rides from strangers, but usually they knew the drivers who stopped, albeit sometimes stretching the admonition on a particularly cold day! Later that day, Daisy was horrified to hear on the radio it was twenty-five below that morning. Usually they listened to weather news early in the day but for some reason had missed the report that morning. However, the chilly walk had not harmed Flora who felt being in school for the Valentine exchange was worth braving the cold.

That spring, Juanita graduated from high school with bleaker prospects for continuing her education than any of her siblings had faced. Like Neil, she knew she would have to remain home another year and was resigned to attending business college in Croquille. This would at least enable her to get a job, eventually in the Twin Cities she fervently hoped, and finally get away from home.

Most young people are eager to leave the nest and strike out on their own, either at college or a job, even if they have been happy at home. It is part of normal growing up, although occasionally some youths, like birds, hesitate and totter on the edge of the familiar doorstep. Juanita's determination to leave was intensified by her knowledge that Daisy was looking forward to, at long last, being alone with her own family.

As often happens in the Midwest, a severe winter was

followed by an exceptionally hot summer and lack of rain. This year's drought made those of previous years seem comparatively mild. No rain fell from mid-May until well into July. The corn never came up and the oats had to be cut for hay as by early July the short stalks had ripened mostly without heads. By the time the first brief rain fell in July, the oat hay had been laboriously pitched by hand to hayrack, then up into the haymow where Flora's task was to pitch and stack it back into the broad spaces separated only by the beams which formed triangles to the chaff-covered haymow floor. The short stalks of oats, dry and harsh, seemed to spew out dirt. And it was at least ninety-five degrees in the haymow. Flora developed a quiet hatred of oat hay. While Herb returned to the field for another load, she cooled herself by washing with cold water in the kitchen, complaining to her sister and mother, who also were trying to withstand the devastating heat which lingered for days.

Although a welcome distraction, the summer's discomfort was somehow made even more stressful by the first visit since their marriage two years ago of Jean and Steve. They occupied the north bedroom which always had been the boys' room, now conveniently vacant, and soon the room was overflowing with clutter.

Their mess grated on Daisy's nerves for though she often did not have the energy to clean as thoroughly as she would have liked because of the heat, she tried hard to keep the house looking neat.

"We'll feel cooler if the house is neat," she often told the girls, and they both tried to follow her example. But the young marrieds were guests and seemingly blind to the disruption they caused in the stifling house.

Steve, following his father's ways, had several ideas for jobs which he assured Herb would bring in good money for the month they were to stay. He used his father-in-law's name as a reference for a sales job of assorted car parts which Herb later heard did not live up to Steve's glowing account.

But what really worried Daisy more than the heat, or her pity for the barren looking future Juanita faced, when she knew she should be entering college, was the fear that Jean and Steve would persuade the graduate to go West with them.

Many a young person upon completing high school has gone to live with a married sibling to get a start in a new community. Family members helping each other was a cherished idea, Daisy knew. But she and Herb, no doubt letting their imagination wander darkly because of the heat and their own pinched circumstances, were sure Juanita would find herself doing field work or other menial jobs from which she could never escape.

Any attempt to rationally point this out to Juanita met with stony resistance, and before the Rankins' visit was over, relations were strained. Juanita naturally turned to her older sister for companionship and they appeared such congenial pals that even Flora, used to being left out, was quite aware of their closeness and also realized her parents' worry.

However, this was one worry which Daisy and Herb need not have added to their daily list, for Juanita did not accompany her sister and brother-in-law out West. Indeed, she had never seriously considered it, for she was aware that once she completed business college, office work would be available.

Neil also came home that summer for a brief visit, full of his new knowledge about electronics which he shared endlessly with anyone who would listen. Flora, who kept asking him what he had brought for her, finally realized he had not brought her anything, after her mother privately pointed this out.

Daisies Don't Tell

Why the child thought he would bring her anything was a mystery as neither brother had ever shown the slightest interest in her; actually they were not overly attentive to their own full sisters. But children are naturally self-centered and eleven year olds tend to feel themselves the center of their universe.

Despite the stresses of the summer, Juanita and Flora had a few times of fun, keeping each other cool by throwing cold water from the well on each other in their bathing suits. Daisy got a snapshot showing Juanita momentarily shivering as her younger sister vigorously threw a pailful of the water, which never lost its blessed chill from the well deep in the hardpan soil.

Daisy had climbed the snowy hill the previous hard winter to photograph the girls in new snow pants she had gotten for each- a most needed item that cold winter. Now she made both girls identical pink cotton dresses, so briefly the age span seemed eclipsed.

Juanita completed the business college course the next school year, and got a job at a granite company office in town, proudly moving into a rented room. Her last year at home was more pleasant with the acquisition of a boyfriend, Ed Logan, who lived on a farm some distance up the county road. They had met in school and the friendship began when he offered her rides home. One Saturday night, when they returned from a movie, while Ed was goodbying in the Norton kitchen, the wind came up and he was vexed to find his car, left by the road because the Norton driveway was partially snow-filled, was now snowed in.

It was nearly midnight and Juanita, fearing to awaken her father who did not like Ed anyway (the senior Logan was an annoying braggart) even though the family was Protestant, chose the lesser of two evils. She told Ed to sleep in Neil's empty room and retired to her own bedroom. When Herb awoke the next morning he was upset to see the Logan car parked at the end of his driveway, though he could readily see why it was still there. He rushed to awaken the unwanted guest and vigorously shoveled and pushed until he got the embarrassed youth on his way home. He trusted his daughter's morals, but he did not want even the appearance of impropriety. Daisy, feeling that Juanita had made the sensible decision, calmed his discussion about the overnight guest. But the next time Neil came home, his father related the incident to him in great detail, concluding "I got that kid's car out of there as soon as I could before any of the Germans saw it!"

While working at her first job, driving a company-owned car, Juanita was involved in a minor accident which was not her fault. Her boss immediately blamed her, but her parents came to her rescue, staunchly supporting their daughter's claim, proving that "blood is thicker than water," as Daisy laughingly said.

She had a series of sayings, which she always prefaced with "As my mother used to say," Typical of late nineteenth-century, middle-America culture, they included "A stitch in time saves nine," "Where cobwebs grow, beaux never go," and "Where there's a will, there's a way," (reflecting the deeply imbedded Puritan work ethic), as well as whimsical sayings such as dropping the dishrag meant company was coming.

Americans in the 1930s were spared hourly television coverage of world problems, but newspapers and radio fully covered major events. In 1936, the Western world was intrigued with the love affair of King Edward VIII of England and his abdication so he could marry the "woman I love"—the American divorcee, Wallis Warfield Simpson. As usual, the two sisters responded according to age, Juanita thinking it was the most romantic happening of the century while Flora's classmates wrote "Wally is nuts" on their workbooks.

The legacy of horrible weather the previous year carried over into 1937. That spring, all three of the Norton horses became ill and died after weeks of lying delirious in their straw beds. The veterinarian blamed their deaths on poisonous weeds which had grown during the dry summer in the wild meadow where Herb had cut hay for some years.

The death of all his horses was not only an emotional blow to Herb, but a financial loss as he had never thought of switching from horse power to a tractor. Babe and Buster, a matched team he had purchased many years earlier, had been a good working team. The third horse, named King, a large Belgian weighing some 1,700 pounds, had been on the place even longer. Herb and Daisy both felt special affection for King as he had been pals with Melba, the last of their purebred Percheron broodmares. When Melba finally had died of old age, King had roamed the farmyard looking for her.

Now as the large Belgian gelding lay comatose, Flora crept into his stall, wordlessly wishing she had some magic to cure him. Like farm children for generations, she wandered alone in the mild spring evening, walking out the unspoken grief she shared with her parents.

Herb felt overwhelmed with blows, first of weather and now losing all the horses, but Daisy, drawing on the hidden inner strength many people never realize they have, encouraged him, saying they'd come out of it.

"We'll make it, Herb, I know we will," she said, and buoyed by her belief in his ability and the thought that "this too shall pass," he returned to the daily grind with new determination. And with the cash from sale of wool from the annual sheep shearing, he was able to purchase a new team, whom they named Lady and Pearl.

Although they had practically no social life, the monotony of unceasing work was softened on Sunday. Daisy enjoyed the time she spent reading to Herb even though he often nodded. In the early years of their marriage, he would even quit work when the Farmer's Weekly came in the mail so she could read the continued stories. They had quit all magazine subscriptions as money became more scarce. Daisy also had quit getting books from the public library; modern books depressed her and she now sought escape through lighter reading. She never would have chosen Western books herself, but she knew they suited Herb. They often spoke wistfully of ever seeing the Great West, though realizing it would hardly resemble Zane Grey's description.

Since she had left home, Carol often bought her parents a book for Christmas or birthday and both she and Jean gave Daisy gift subscriptions to Good Housekeeping and Ladies' Home Journal. She often read stories in those periodicals aloud also. One, in particular, spoke to her oft depressed feelings.

When asked why she had told her maid to prepare chicken and ice cream for dinner-what was she celebrating? The heroine answered "Because it's another day."

"I just must take life a day at a time," Daisy continuously told herself. Herb kept reassuring her she eventually would feel better. He means better physically, she thought. I just can't explain to him how blue I sometimes feel.

The extreme drought of 1936 also had brought an infestation of Russian thistles to the Norton's sheep pasture, a weed previously unknown in that area. Canadian thistles had always been a problem, with Herb convinced that old Fritz Behler scattered the seed on his land despite not having the slightest proof.

But the Russian thistle obviously was a product of the

drought. Herb offered to pay Flora a nickel for every hundred of the large round plants she would pull. At first, it was fun to count the plants as she accumulated them. Then she realized that twenty times five cents equals a dollar: if she pulled twenty hundred-a discouraging 2,000 thistles!-she would earn a whole dollar.

Daisy thought Herb was indulging in slave labor, taking clear advantage of their child's interest in helping him outside, as if in perverse contrast to her brothers. But she had to admit it did the child no harm to pull the offending thistles. One night when Flora was busy earning another nickel as twilight faded into darkness out in the sheep pasture, her mother climbed the hill to find her, bringing along several of the freshly baked cupcakes she frequently made. Flora, struck by her thoughtfulness, consciously realized, perhaps for the first time, how much her mother must love her to walk out into the pasture with the fresh cakes. She realized that Daisy never walked anywhere; strolling for exercise was unheard of for, in addition to Daisy's weight, she like all housewives was on her feet "exercising" all day long.

That summer, Floyd unexpectedly came home for a visit, supposedly to tell his parents that the previous December he had married Oleta Stevens, a Wisconsin girl he had met at Graylin. The marriage had, of necessity, been kept secret or she would have had to leave college, as no married students were allowed. After a long struggle with finances and a bout of illness, he had received his bachelor's degree the previous summer. Daisy would always feel a little bitter about that incident. A postcard had arrived in their rural mailbox the morning of graduation day. Floyd had carelessly sent it off at the last minute-undoubtedly urged by Oleta. When Daisy read it, and realized the commencement ceremony was that very afternoon, she immediately dropped everything and decided to drive to St.

Paul. With luck she would arrive in time for the ceremony. She would stay overnight with her old school friend, Connie Rempel, who had a lovely home on Summit Avenue in St. Paul.

Ignoring the obvious lack of thoughtfulness to inform his parents earlier of this important event, Daisy amazed the girls by efficiently packing an overnight case and after Herb hurriedly cleaned the car, she was on her way.

Herb mentally berated his oldest son for his lack of consideration for not realizing that his graduation from her alma mater meant a great deal to Daisy. It was worth the hurried trip to her to once again be on campus and see her favorite, if problematic, nephew graduate. And if Floyd was not ecstatic in seeing his aunt, he was at least polite. He did not introduce Oleta and Daisy was unaware of her.

Now he was home for a week's visit. When Floyd left at the end of the week, his parents were still unaware of his marriage. Somehow he had not wanted, or been able to tell them. Carol, now living in a Minneapolis suburb, heard rumors of the marriage from mutual friends of her brother and so the news gradually filtered into his parents' consciousness.

18

Daisy's dream of being home alone with her own family—Herb and their child—had come true at last. But her enjoyment of the long anticipated time was clouded by her continuing poor health. And even more unfortunately, the poor health, while it had some physical causes, was primarily mental.

Daisy suffered depression, at a time when the word was known only as referring to the poor economic condition of the country. No one was aware that mental depression can make a hell out of heaven, to use Milton's words.

The Norton in-laws, especially, were baffled as to Daisy's condition, for she looked healthy and appeared normal. Like most relatives, they decided she was either lazy or just eccentric, particularly about her sleeping late mornings.

And whatever a sister-in-law said, no matter how innocently, assumed a negative meaning to Daisy. Part of the insidious characteristics of depression is that the sufferer, often feeling guilty over inability to accomplish tasks, is defensive, keeping the proverbial chip on her shoulder.

With no neighbors or close friends nearby and her only sister unsympathetic to her problems, Daisy's main social contacts were occasional visits from Norton relatives. Linnie often would drive to the farm on Sunday afternoon, bringing flowers from her garden, which thrived because she had city water. Knowing Daisy was both unable to tend flowers and the drought had killed what she did plant, it was thoughtful of her. However, her bouquets invariably were zinnias, a harsh, garish flower which Daisy secretly came to hate, although she never would have dreamed of telling Linnie that.

When Herb's much admired oldest brother, John, and his wife, Bertie, stopped to see the Nortons one summer afternoon, Bertie innocently commented on the many empty canning jars in the basement, which she had noticed on her trip to the toilet closet. It was perhaps not a tactful remark, but how often are in-law comments tactful? And it served to infuriate Daisy: first with self-disgust that she was not able to fill the jars as she once did and, secondly, at her hapless sister-in-law's audacity in mentioning the subject, which only made Daisy feel worse.

These inner furies Daisy never expressed-except in milder retold versions of them sometimes passed on to her daughter who somehow was given the insight to "let them go in one ear and out the other," another of her mother's sayings.

Juanita, who had moved to Minneapolis, showed her concern for Daisy by coming home frequently on weekends, often bringing some small item, such as grapefruit, which she knew her mother could not afford. After she had left home and her own life expanded with congenial work and social contacts, Juanita began to realize the terrible toll that isolation and ill health were taking on her mother's spirits.

A new family had moved into the next place up the main road from the Nortons. Flora met several of the girls who were near her own age one day while opening the gate Herb had installed in the Mississippi River pasture to allow the cattle to go down to the river to drink.

The children easily began visiting and through joint urging of their mothers, obtained permission for them all to go swimming or to at least play in the river that afternoon. Daisy, ever fearful of the treachery of the Father of Waters, even though it was now low with feeble current, came and sat on the bank and chatted politely with the girls' mother. She turned out to be a much harried woman who already had eight children and would give birth to four more. Her husband was ill and seldom worked, and of course they were Catholic.

Herb and Daisy had much to say in private, often at mealtime with Flora listening, about poor families having so many children, conveniently forgetting that a decade earlier, people probably had said the same about them.

Flora was happy to have chums her own age and she spent many happy hours with the three girls, Dorothy, Donna, and Clara, each a year apart. The girls liked to come to the Norton home, probably to avoid their noisy smaller siblings. They played Parcheesi on the front porch, went swimming in the less dangerous Soo River, and liked to sing popular songs while Flora played the piano. Sometimes Daisy even played the piano for their harmonizing. The girls also began to borrow books from Daisy's collection and Dorothy always credited Mrs. Norton for helping her develop the love of reading.

But while the Bissette family provided companionship for her daughter, it did nothing to relieve Daisy's isolation. She could not bring herself to go visit Mrs. Bissette, though Flora had told her the lady liked to read, thinking that would provide a common bond. Even if she felt well, Daisy would have recoiled at visiting a house she knew could be nothing but noise and confusion. And with her depression, she could barely keep her own house running.

The Croquille Public School system that summer instituted an instrumental music program and Daisy was determined to give her child an advantage she never had. Flora, now 12, could walk into town three times weekly for lessons on a violin they rented from the school. Daisy dreamed fondly of the girl someday playing solos. But while Flora was conscientious about practicing, she did not become a soloist, though she appreciated the out-of-town trips membership in the orchestra brought during high school.

Other than her pleasure in affording her daughter this cultural advantage (she always had been unhappy that they could not afford piano lessons for her), Daisy's life was a dull blur. Now that the family was down to just two other people and she should have had time to develop her own interests, she seemingly had no interests to develop. She often wondered if she would lose her mind, aware of mental instability in her brother, Sid, who continued his bitter, lonely life on his farm. The last time she and Herb had visited him, he had cursed his fate, along with the drought.

However, though she was often blue or depressed, Daisy never lost touch with reality and lovingly followed Flora's activities as well as news the other children wrote home. When Flora was asked to recite the 100th Psalm as part of the annual Children's Day program at church, Daisy wanted to buy the girl a new pair of black slippers, as the patent leather dress shoes were called. Wondering if she should spend the money, she walked up along the foot of the hillside west of the buildings which curved around and then opened into the back fields to confer with Herb who was cultivating corn. He assured her it was all right.

"If she needs the shoes, get them," he told his wife. So she happily returned to the yard to tell the good news to Flora, who was struck with how important the new shoes seemed to her mother. Although she always enjoyed having new dresses her mother made, Flora had not really been aware she needed new shoes.

The children all wrote home frequently, except Floyd, and she kept their letters each in a separate cubbyhole in the Larkin desk she had inherited from her mother. Flora Jane had won it as a premium before her marriage in 1866 for selling Larkin products by team and buggy. Daisy said they were similar to Watkins products-flavoring and spices-now brought to farm homes by a salesman driving an old car.

As if her own emotional low, aggravated by both physical problems as well as "change of life" (as menopause was then delicately described) were not enough, the national news further depressed her.

The Nortons, like most loyal Republicans, felt sure FDR's efforts to solve the nation's ills with widely expanded use of the federal government and the ever proliferating alphabet agencies which kept appearing, would ruin the country.

Herb and Daisy had taken to discussing politics and current events at mealtime since, with only one child who had no one to fight with, adult conversation was again possible. Flora used to tell her friends "We often had roast FDR for dinner."

Since they had been able to retain their home and had their small but steady milk income, the Nortons could not see the benefit of the most visible New Deal agencies such as the Works Progress Administration and the Civilian Conservation Corps. Like farmers everywhere, used to hustling from dawn to dark, Herb often joked that "WPA" stood for "We poke along." It disgusted him to pass working sites where several men seemed to do nothing but lean on their shovels.

A young man from the CCC had drowned in the Mississippi River that past summer while the unit was camped near Soo Falls en route to Eagle Falls. He must have been drunk, Daisy and Herb agreed, else why would a young man drown as low as the river was there?

What bothered them more was the talk Herb had heard in town before the 1936 election. "They told the WPA fellows the Friday before the election, 'Put up your shovels, for if FDR isn't reelected, there won't be any more work for you,'" Herb reported. And the incumbent president had been reelected by a landslide, with only two states going GOP. Of course, like most second-hand reports, he had no way of verifying the truth of such statements. But they were widely believed by the president's many critics.

In November of 1937, the Nortons received a telegram announcing the birth of their first grandchild-a girl to Steve and Jean, who had named her Myrtice Jean. Flora felt very important hurrying out to the barn after they received the news via phone to inform her dad he was now a grandfather. Two months later, John and Carol also had a daughter, named Myrtice Susan. Daisy understood why both girls had named their daughters after their own mother, but she thought from a practical angle, it was well that the Rankins were out West to avoid name confusion.

That summer of 1938, Daisy felt extremely tired and rested every afternoon. Flora, scarcely aware of her mother's depression as Daisy was always up and got meals, with minimal help from her daughter, found her mother's rest time meant she was free to go swimming with her friends. In addition to the Bissette girls, she had established an enduring friendship with Florence Johnson, another only child whose parents lived down the road on the narrow peninsula of land between the two rivers.

Florence was four years older and already had a steady boyfriend whom she saw on Sundays, but Flora was content to do her own lunch dishes, then go to the Johnsons and help Florence with hers, so they could swim. Now that she was older, Flora was allowed to swim in a millpond upstream in the Soo River. This small cement dam which forced the river water into a long canal to power a feed mill was at the edge of the Norton property. It served as the rural community's social center in summer.

Suddenly a letter from Floyd broke Flora's idyllic schedule. He was bringing his wife and her parents to meet his family. And, would they please have Juanita, now working in Minneapolis for Bell Telephone Company, and Carol and John there too, so Oleta could met them all at one time?

To her daughter's chagrin, Daisy immediately quit resting each afternoon and pressed Flora into helping her clean the entire house. Now the girl became aware of how ashamed her mother really was of their lack of indoor plumbing. The morning of the visit, Daisy filled her old-fashioned pitcher on her chiffonier in her upstairs bedroom with water, and laid out her daintiest towels. She knew the women would need to use the basement toilet after their arrival, but she felt she could not have them wash their hands in the kitchen where last minute dinner details would create confusion.

But the guests didn't bother to go upstairs and thus ate dinner without washing their hands after using the rustic "restroom"- something which Daisy told Flora she would never have done.

It was a pleasant visit, despite the strain of a young wife meeting all her husband's family en masse-undoubtedly why she had brought her own parents along. Oleta was an only child and she proved to be genuinely interested in Floyd's family as the years passed.

Flora thought she and her two sisters, all dressed, appropriately she felt, in summer dresses as it was late August and still warm, must have seemed country bumpkins by the guests since Oleta and her mother were in fall apparel.

The next day after the big event, Daisy returned to her afternoon rest and Flora thankfully joined her friends at the swimming hole. Now that she was a teenager, Floyd, whom she scarcely remembered being at home, seemed a stranger to her.

Perhaps the Stevens' visit was good for Daisy's emotional health, for her depression lifted for a time and she decided to invite friends and relatives to a party-the main attraction being to eat watermelon since the watermelons Herb had planted that year had provided a bumper crop. Inspired briefly to use her long-latent literary ability, Daisy wrote the invitations in jingle form:

"On September nine, we Nortons will stand,

And give to you all a right welcoming hand."

In addition to the time, she penned a personal note to some of the relatives on her own side. But Bill and Eva Pepin, who had celebrated their golden wedding anniversary that year, understandably were too old to venture that far at night. John Baldwin's parents, whom Daisy particularly felt she should invite, had another engagement, as did another couple from her teaching days.

But Carol, knowing the disappointment her mother would feel and that she perhaps would not believe the excuses were legitimate, made a special effort to drive up that night with John and their baby. Daisy felt grateful to the busy young mother for making the effort. While Carol had had her differences with Daisy when growing up, both shared a strong sense of family loyalty. When Carol became ill with an ear infection during her nurse's training, Daisy had gone to Minneapolis to care for her.

Daisy also planned a second melon party for the Nortons and here she need not worry about excuses. Everyone came, even cousin Ray Norton's brother, Orrie, his wife Opal, and her little sister who had been in Flora's class in Soo Rapids. These last three had not been invited simply because Daisy had never even thought of them as they seldom saw each other.

"We just told them all the Nortons were invited," Linnie laughingly explained when she and Jim arrived, along with Alta, home for one of her frequent weekend visits to her parents. And for once, Daisy did not let three unexpected guests upset her. After all, there was plenty of watermelon.

After visiting in the usually quiet parlor, the guests gathered around the expanded kitchen table to enjoy the fresh melons.

As the evening closed Jim jokingly said, "I've got to get these women out of here before they start getting rid of the water in these melons."

Later that fall, Steve and Jean drove back to Minnesota to visit their relatives and with cooler weather and no worry about their taking anyone else out West, for Daisy the visit was more pleasant than their last one.

Like many young mothers, Jean now was interested in taking home some of her long unused things such as her old doll buggy and on the last day of the visit, she had Daisy ransacking the house to find items. When they left, everything was topsy-turvy.

Steve, realizing what a mess they were leaving, apologized, but Jean gaily said, "We have to leave you something." She, like other relatives, was oblivious to Daisy's real condition and that she had been going only on nerves during the past days.

When the Rankins drove out of the yard, Daisy sank wearily into bed.

19

Even though Daisy was far from well and her daughter caught but rare glimpses of the merry person she could be when feeling good, life during her junior high years was pleasant for Flora. As she was now old enough to realize, she had the advantage of both being an only child, with money not quite so scarce, and also the benefit of attention from her older sisters.

Daisy had told her daughter about her Aunt Myrtice's death and how she and the child's grandmother had moved to the farm from St. Paul. While she refrained from mentioning her delicate relationship with Herb, she confided to Flora that her college degree had "stuck in your father's craw for a long time." The fact that Myrtice, too, had a degree didn't seem to alter Daisy's conviction. She made no effort to be tactful about her perceived grievances with the Campbells. Flora wondered if most women have troubled relations with their in-laws. While Aunt Linnie and Uncle Jim (who sometimes handed her a bag of cookies when she was in the bakery with her father) had always been kind and hospitable to her, she felt she knew what her mother was talking about.

Once, when Flora was staying overnight with the

Campbells, as she occasionally did to attend some special school event, she was in an upstairs bedroom where her aunt and cousin Alta were critically examining a stylish hat Linnie's daughter-in-law, Violet, had laid on the bed. Violet, a sweet-mannered woman, was married to the Campbells' only son, Don, and for years they lived in a tiny house right behind the bakery-a house obviously owned by the senior Campbells.

Flora remembered Alta lifting the offending hat, apparently looking for a price tag. Unable to find one, she said, "I wonder what she paid for this?" Young as she was, Flora knew Alta was really saying, in effect, that her flighty sister-in-law was wasting family money since Don's livelihood came from the bakery.

Flora sometimes marveled that her half sisters/cousins even liked her for she had come to realize how much her mother had favored her, try as Daisy might to be fair. But Carol had both her younger sisters visit her summers, one at a time, and Jean had asked Flora to stay overnight occasionally with her when she was living at the Campbells. Now that Juanita was working in the Twin Cities, she always had Flora stay with her over the weekends when the Croquille orchestra came to the state music festival at the University of Minnesota campus in Minneapolis.

Juanita now had a new boyfriend, Leo Whitehead, who gallantly drove across town to pick Flora up after the last music meet. Perhaps more important, Juanita bought her younger sister birthday gifts she otherwise never would have had. For her fourteenth birthday Flora was elated when Juanita gave her a bright cotton print housecoat. It was not an expensive item, but she felt almost elegant wearing it that evening reading the new book her mother had given her. Carol, too, faithfully gave her youngest sister books for birthdays and Christmas.

While their daughter was busy finding her place in a large

junior high school with a comforting reprieve Sundays in church school, Daisy and Herb were increasingly aware of the trouble brewing in Europe. They listened in horror to daily radio reports of Hitler's advances and the fruitless efforts of British Prime Minister Neville Chamberlain to "find peace in our time."

When the Nazis invaded Poland in the fall of 1939, they found they actually agreed with FDR in promoting the lend-lease program. Once Flora, repeating her parents' ideas of giving all possible aid to England, was told scathingly by an upper classman, "You must be an interventionist." Isolationism was rife in the Midwest.

Labor Day Weekend. both Juanita, who brought a girl-friend, and Neil, proudly driving a new car he had purchased, came home. Flora, who had been swimming at the millpond when he arrived, was rather startled when she got back to the farmhouse and found him sitting on the back porch, asking where Dad was.

"My dad is up in the field," she said, realizing after she'd spoken that it was HIS father too and she should have said "our" dad. But she was too embarrassed to mention it.

Apparently Juanita had outgrown being ashamed of her parents' lack of modern conveniences, or felt her friend would understand. While both Neil and Juanita were busily building their own lives in Chicago and Minneapolis, their visits provided special times for Flora and relieved the otherwise barren social life of her parents.

Neil surprised Daisy the next spring by sending Flora twelve pieces of popular sheet music, some of them oldies such as "When It's Spring Time in the Rockies." Daisy was very pleased that when Neil came home, he liked to sing to his little sister's accompaniment. Both were very amateur but it gave them a common bond, for the first time.

That spring of 1940 as Hitler's armies moved steadily unchecked through eastern Europe, Herb was annoyed when Ray Behler, now farming his dad's old place next to the Nortons, openly bragged about the Nazi leader. He would come over to see Herb on some pretext, then sit with his motor running in his pickup, as if ready to leave, while he gleefully recounted the German victories.

"That darn German just comes over here so he can brag about Hitler," Herb told Daisy. All the years of exchanging farm work notwithstanding, Ray's praise of Hitler deepened the Nortons' dislike of German-Americans. But none of the other farmers vocalized their admiration of the Fuhrer, if indeed they had any.

One day, Herb came home from taking the cream to Soo Falls, upset over a worse aspect of Hitler's regime. A storekeeper of Jewish background was worrying himself literally sick, Herb said, over what was happening to his relatives in Germany. While it was apparent to Americans who gave the situation any thought that the Jews were being persecuted, the horrifying scope of Hitler's genocide policies were not yet generally known.

Like many congenial couples, Herb and Daisy, as they grew older, came to hold similar views on current events. Once, though, when she said she would have voted for Woodrow Wilson had women then been able to vote, Herb had irritated her by retorting, "Why, he was nothing but a darned Democrat!"

They shared the ingrained prejudice against Catholicism, while feeling no personal animosity for individuals of that faith. Herb, in fact, enjoyed his relationship with the farmers with

Daisies Don't Tell

whom he exchanged harvest work, developing even a rather detached, fatherly relationship with young Behler, now farming his father's place.

Once, during silo threshing time, Ray asked Herb to call him early in the morning to be sure he got up on time. The phone call failed to arouse Ray or his wife, but when Herb went to the Soo River pasture, adjoining the Behlers, to bring in the cows, his barking dog set the Behler dog barking and that awakened Ray. So the younger man said Herb really got him up one way or another!

Daisy's lack of contact with the farm wives was based as much upon her inability to make small talk with them as any feeling of ill will. Carol was sure Daisy felt herself superior to the neighbor women, but Flora tried to explain to her big sister it really was because her mother was at a loss for conversation. "I just don't know what in the world I'd talk about with them," she told her daughter.

In May, Daisy, feeling one of her periodic surges of energy, decided to drive down to Elk Grove and attend the high school graduation of her late brother Gene's youngest son. He was graduating from her old high school and she and Flora would stay with Eva.

Age had not really mellowed Eva's outlook on life, but since Daisy no longer was in danger of having to ask her for any help, they maintained a friendly rapport. Flora thought their house, which Uncle Billy had built, very elegant with its built-in china closet and artificial fruit in a tall compote.

As she was driving home the next day Daisy, sharing her inner thoughts as mothers like to do with their daughters, remarked how she now wanted to donate any extra energy she had beyond caring for Herb and the house to helping her old friend, Blanch, who was getting on in years.

Flora listened respectfully, but inwardly wondered how much extra energy her mother would ever have to help anyone.

Later that summer, Daisy had a special treat when her first cousin, Myra Snow, visited. A maiden lady, as old maids were charitably called, Myra was a missionary to China, now home on furlough. She and Daisy talked steadily for a solid day and evening of old times growing up near Elk Grove, their shared relatives, and especially of Myra's work teaching in a school run by the Methodists in Tienstin. Myra's mother, Ada, was a sister to Daisy's father and Daisy's middle name was for this aunt.

Daisy had often dreamed of becoming a missionary when she was young. However, fate had always kept her from it-first there was her mother to provide for and then Myrtice's children.

As Myra talked professionally about her school, Daisy sensed the social status the missionaries unconsciously portrayed. They were there to teach, and convert the Chinese, but hardly to share equally with them socially. Before Myra left the next day, after expressing enjoyment to again sleep in a farmhouse upstairs room, Daisy felt her life had probably been as useful as her cousin's, despite her pinched economic conditions. And she couldn't help but smile at Herb's remark that "No wonder Myra is a missionary-she's so bossy no one would ever marry her!"

That summer, Flora got her first job-picking strawberries for a neighbor, and later mowing the huge lawn of Ben Ickler who had purchased several acres in the Mississippi River pasture. She also earned money for school selling corn to business people in Soo Falls.

By now, nearly all that pasture had been sold for building lots, creating a small colony of commuters to Croquille. Most of them were Catholic, and while Herb and Flora had pleasant discourse with them in business encounters, they remained distant to Daisy.

Ickler was not Catholic—he didn't mention attending any church—and as Herb had continued dealings with him, digging his basement and other odd jobs, he found him bright and congenial. So he suggested to Daisy it would be nice to invite Ben for Sunday dinner, along with his wife, who worked in the Twin Cities but occasionally came up for weekends.

It was the first time he had ever urged any social activity and she knew it would be good to have company, but she could not face the idea of inviting a stranger who might not want to come to a house without a bathroom. And she had never met the woman.

"If we had them, they'd have to have us back, and we just don't have the clothes and money to keep up with them," she told Herb, trying to sound sensible, while rationalizing to herself that she really did not have the energy or nerve to try to make friends with this couple, obviously sophisticated and used to the Twin Cities.

Herb agreed and no more was said. Mention of what it might cost for company meals, and entertaining extras, was enough to silence him. But Flora, hearing the conversation, thought it too bad her mother didn't feel up to occasional social life.

Summers were particularly pleasant for the farm girl for she enjoyed helping her dad outside. She enjoyed the friendly joking of her parents, especially on their different recollection of a verse of poetry. Aware, as many farmers are, of the beauty of nature, Herb early taught his daughter to appreciate the sunsets. Seeing one, he would quote a long remembered line:

"Count that day lost, when the slow descending sun
   Sees from thy hand, no noble action done."

Flora naturally mentioned the lines to her mother who said it went somewhat differently, but no matter; now in the relative quiet of their small family, all three Nortons had time to savor one of the sometimes forgotten advantages of rural life.

Unlikely as it might seem in their straight-laced, hard-working life, both Herb and Daisy had some interest in poetry. It was natural for Daisy as a former English teacher, while Herb apparently absorbed some literary interest by osmosis.

"I got educated being married to two Coolidge girls," he often laughed to Flora.

She had discovered, tucked in the parlor bookcases, a copy of Washington Irving's Sketch Book which Daisy had given her father when he graduated from the University Farm School in 1908. She had primly written "Congratulations" in it, putting her initials in tiny letters at the bottom of the page.

And all through the years, Daisy had treasured Farm Rhymes by James Whitcomb Riley, which Herb had given her upon her graduation from college that same year, though she was quite aware that Myrtie had probably suggested the gift.

Obviously they had neither time nor inclination to sit around reciting poetry and what reading Daisy did had narrowed to light fiction, but the now forgotten books were another bond between them. However, the older children probably felt the subject had little impact on their parents' daily lives.

That spring, Flora helped shovel gravel with Herb, who was doing some county road work, and Daisy was disgusted when Flora told her several of the neighbor women had cautioned her about the heavy work she was doing.

Florence's mother, a large, kindly, but uneducated woman,

had told her that she would have "female trouble" later by doing such heavy farm work, although the heaviest item Flora ever pitched was hay. She never handled corn or grain bundles. But the shoveling of dirt on the county road seemed to worry several of the women. Daisy, as usual, was affronted that these neighbors with so little education should offer advice to her daughter who was strong and healthy, and obviously enjoyed working with her dad.

Farm prices had improved and while the Nortons were far from rich, they could occasionally take money for small luxuries, such as fruit or even a large candy bar which Daisy judiciously broke into small pieces for Flora each day, her loving gesture having helped over the years to create many cavities in the girl's mouth.

Through long habit of having no money for preventive medical or dental care, Daisy never had taken any of the children for dental checkups. Now, she realized she should have done so and Flora was chagrined to find she had many cavities. She had learned to ride Floyd's old "wheel" and so had to spend most of one Easter holiday biking to dental appointments.

Despite her many cavities, Flora had long been uncomfortably aware that even when she was small, her mother had painstakingly eked out nickels for a Hershey bar for her, but never for Juanita or Neil. (She could not remember the older three siblings living at home.) She was amazed when Neil told her he had eaten an entire candy bar at one time while on an outing. Flora was never allowed more than a square or two at a time but she knew the candy represented her mother's love and also skillful stretching of her pennies.

Now there was no reason to feel guilty about having candy and, with less economic stress for her parents, Flora happily divided her time helping her dad and swimming with her friends. She and Herb both knew Daisy was not well, but when one is not in bed with a fever, or actual physical manifestations, it is easy to put the problem out of mind.

One day in July, the rural community was stunned to learn that Buddy Gustafson, the little boy with whom Flora used to play, now eleven years old, had been struck by a car while riding his bike to see a friend. A priest was called, but before he arrived, the boy was dead.

Madeline, his mother, a devout Catholic, was comforted because the body was still warm when her priest arrived, she told Daisy who had gone to offer her sympathy. The difference in religion made no difference to Daisy in her concern for another woman losing her only child. The tragedy brought back all her own sorrow at losing Ada Beryl.

She felt she and Flora must attend the funeral, which was to be held in the cathedral in Croquille. Knowing she would feel uneasy as a Protestant in a Catholic church, Daisy suggested that Flora see if Mrs. Johnson would accompany them to the funeral.

As she sat uncomfortably through the Catholic liturgy, Daisy tried hard to keep her mind on asking God's grace for the bereaved parents, and put aside her disgust for the constant bowing and scraping, as she thought of the parishioners' devout kneeling. But she also was struck with the universality of grief.

20

Jean and Steve returned to Minnesota again that summer, but they rented a place in town as Steve was taking summer school classes. He was trying to finish his college education and Jean confided to Flora, who had biked in to visit her sister, that he hoped someday to be a college professor, even president. Herb and Daisy had to admire his gumption and felt he would "make something of himself."

Jean had hoped to drive her mother and Flora on outings throughout the summer, but soon she too found that shrinking finances meant foregoing buying extra gas. Flora enjoyed having her oldest niece, now nearly three, out to the farm where she took her for a brief ride on the hayrack.

Later that summer, Daisy was surprised one afternoon to have Floyd, Oleta, and her mother drive unexpectedly into the yard. This visit lacked all the stress of the previous one, since it was unexpected, but Daisy, inwardly horrified about how dusty and shabby the house looked, went into chills.

Now Mrs. Stevens, a tall, commanding looking woman with a somewhat haughty manner, showed her true colors. She might be an upper-class social leader in her hometown in

Wisconsin where her husband was a respected dentist, but she was a kind woman. She insisted on wrapping Daisy in the light coat she had with her and showed only sincere sympathy for Daisy's nervous plight.

Oleta, too, wore a coat which she kept on throughout the visit, but for a different reason. She was expecting her first baby that December and was not ready to announce it. She and Floyd were moving to Michigan, where Floyd had a position in a university library.

Carol, with her nurse's training, was aware that Daisy needed medical attention, primarily repair work on her uterus which had never been right since her first unsuccessful birth. She kept telling Daisy to come to her hospital, which had excellent doctors.

Without any cash reserve for such an expenditure, Daisy kept postponing the inevitable.

The next fall, Neil announced he was marrying Sally Ofrio, an Italian girl in Chicago. His parents had never met her but by now, with all of their "first" family scattered, it didn't seem too shocking. They learned her family had been Catholic, but after immigrating to this country had abandoned the faith of their fathers.

Juanita also was going to marry the following February. She and Leo already were deep into plans for a large church wedding at the Baptist church in Minneapolis which the Whiteheads attended. The plans also called for what Daisy considered a most elaborate reception. Flora was to help serve. Daisy privately thought her sister should have asked Flora to play her violin, but she said nothing.

Before the fall was over, Daisy had to follow Carol's advice and go to Asbury Hospital in Minneapolis for what turned out to be a hysterectomy. Because she had been in poor health for so long, she was months getting back on her feet so Flora learned, of necessity, to cook, and every Saturday to do the wash and clean house.

Traces of cancer cells were found belatedly in the pathological tests, but no mention was made of need for further treatment. Daisy made Herb promise not to mention the discovery to Flora.

"She has enough to worry about, doing the housework and going to school," she said. Herb privately thought their daughter seemed to be surviving her added responsibilities without undue concern, but he agreed to pacify his wife.

After she was able to leave the hospital, Daisy still was not strong enough to care for herself and Carol, realizing what a dreary existence she would return to at home with Herb and Flora gone most of the day, asked her mother-in-law if she would have Daisy stay there until she was able to care for herself.

The Baldwins, having several empty bedrooms in their nice old house near the Twin Cities, graciously agreed. Herb and Flora came to visit one weekend and after several weeks, Daisy returned home.

Unlike younger women, who now are expected to bounce back within a month after this surgery, Daisy did not feel like herself till nearly spring.

That December 7, which was a Sunday, they had turned the radio off while eating dinner after Flora returned from church, so they missed the initial report of the surprise Japanese attack on Pearl Harbor. But by evening, they were intently listening to the shocking reports.

Whether or not they agreed with some of FDR's worst critics that he secretly was relieved to have the attack occur since that was the only way to change the isolationists' views, they realized this was an historic moment.

The next day Flora and her classmates crowded into the school library to hear the president read his Declaration of War. The immediate effect within the family was that Juanita's wedding plans dissolved. As soon as the news came, Leo told her he knew he would have to fight and he might as well volunteer so he could be in the Air Force. Within weeks, he left for basic training.

That Christmas, Neil brought his new wife to the farm and the city-bred girl thought it quite an adventure. She stood rather in awe of Juanita, now a sophisticated, urbane young lady, and Carol, who also came for the day with John and their now two little girls. As a nurse and mother, the eldest sister was remarkably organized and efficient.

But Sally felt at home with Flora, who was younger and not in any way threatening to the young wife. Flora sensed how she felt about the other sisters and was especially friendly to her.

There is nothing nicer than having houseguests for Christmas, and despite the lack of modern conveniences, that Christmas was a bright one for the Nortons. After their return to Chicago, Sally wrote to thank her mother-in-law, using an ungrammatical phrase as she described their drive home. Flora, very conscious of speaking properly, as Daisy always corrected her if she didn't, immediately pounced on the error.

But Daisy said kindly, "She hasn't had enough schooling to know that what she wrote was wrong. Don't blame her."

By spring, Daisy was feeling like her old self and during May when Minnesota weather makes one forget the hard winters, she was often up at 5 A.M. busily starting her day's work. That spring, the Nortons traded their old Hudson for a much newer car-a Dodge which was only five years old. It was the newest car Flora ever remembered her parents having and she was quite impressed, especially after a neighbor boy, whose parents had bought a lot directly across the road from the Norton driveway, also seemed impressed.

The first Sunday they had the vehicle, they naturally went for a ride and narrowly avoided what to Daisy would have been humiliation in front of her in-laws. The car motor coughed and, fearing it would stall, Herb slowed down to stop. Seeing that they were right across from the bakery, Daisy cried, "For goodness sake, don't stop here! We don't want the Campbells to see that our car isn't working." So Herb kept going a few blocks and the motor soon was purring smoothly. Flora knew that even the slightest indication that they were incompetent in relatives' eyes was abhorrent to her mother.

She was aware that in a more important area her parents had a real accomplishment to their credit, one that had seemed unattainable ten years ago. They had completed paying off their mortgage through the continued sale of residential lots in the Mississippi pasture. Their original 120 acres were now down to less than 100, but there still was pasture left along the Soo River, and it was all theirs, free and clear. Herb even was able to replace a few modest pieces of horse-drawn machinery. Tractors were coming into general use, but he was not interested in them.

The couple often planned privately, while their daughter was at school, that once she graduated, they could sell the farm and have enough money to buy a house in the Cities, as Minnesotans often refer to their two major metropolitan areas competing on either side of the Mississippi. Herb expected to get work at the University Farm School campus and Daisy thought longingly of being able to live where she could feel comfortable with her neighbors-and have electricity and a bathroom. But they said nothing to Flora, who was just finishing her junior year.

The spring also brought romantic news from an unlikely source. At forty-one years, Cousin Alta was getting married. Neil had joked about her "new papa," since Andy, a genial judge in his hometown where Alta long had taught in northern Minnesota, was gray-haired and older than she.

Her sister-in-law, Violet, dutifully gave a shower for Alta in the new home she and Don had moved into recently. Daisy who identified with the much criticized daughter-in-law, was glad she no longer had to live in her in-laws' backyard, so to speak, since the Campbells' spacious house was just across the alley from their bakery.

Both Daisy and Flora were invited to the shower and Flora felt very grown-up sitting primly with her mother and other ladies from the church. As they were leaving and Alta was receiving best wishes at the doorway, Daisy was amused to see Mrs. Blake, a stalwart of the church, delicately asking Alta's help in getting a teaching job for her daughter. Alta assured her she would try to help. Now that she was older, Daisy could admit that Alta was a most capable person and probably had always meant well.

The war now moved closer to the Norton farm. Neil had been drafted and even though he was reluctant to leave Sally, who did not see how she could manage without him, he was but one of many men whose lives were disrupted by World War II. He brought his car back to the farm from Chicago, put it up on blocks in one end of the machinery shed, and indicated to his dad that if he didn't return, he wanted him to keep the vehicle.

"I think he really meant he didn't want Sally's brothers to have it," Herb told Daisy. The last night before Neil left, the Campbells came out to bid him farewell and Flora realized, with the newfound awe that was happening throughout the country, they might never see him again.

Uncle Jim, with the tears in his eyes magnified by his thick glasses, pumped Neil's hand nervously, muttering "God bless you." Now there were two family members, counting Juanita's fiancé, in the service.

And soon Leo was part of the family. In June, the Nortons received a long letter from Juanita, who had gone to Arizona to be nearby when Leo completed officers' training, informing them that they were now married. The brief civil ceremony was a far cry from the nice church wedding she had planned. She added a sentimental postscript to her little sister who was now "the official Miss Norton," the new bride wrote.

All of Myrtie's children now had chosen mates, and seemingly were happy, Daisy thought thankfully.

Later that summer, she felt she could afford to have the walls of the parlor, sitting room, and the open stairway and upstairs hall wallpapered. The addition of the soft-patterned paper instead of the dreary calcimined walls she had lived with for two decades boosted her spirits.

At times, Flora thought briefly about remaining on the farm to help her dad, unaware that her mother was eagerly looking forward to leaving it. She even had a serious talk with Herb about raising horses that spring when the sweet wild apple blossoms perfuming the pastures made her believe she could live there forever.

But like the blossoms which quickly fade, these thoughts were soon superseded by the knowledge that she wanted to attend college and must move away to find a life of her own.

21

Daisy was disappointed and angry that Flora was not rewarded for her ability in her senior year, as her doting mother felt she should be. She was given no important post on the school paper even though she had made top grades in journalism. But Flora understood perfectly the reason: the male teacher, whom she secretly felt resembled Clark Gable with an oversized macho personality, had been unimpressed with her, perhaps sensing her uncomplimentary appraisal.

Daisy was glad her daughter could be philosophical about what she considered a slap in the face, but then, she sighed, "She's young."

But she was even more incensed that Flora was never selected for the National Honor Society. Flora also felt she knew why, even though she had always been on the honor roll. She had transferred herself from her college preparatory English class to another teacher's class at semester break so she could take a sheet metal course offered from 3 to 6 P.M. daily. With this training, the girls were assured they would easily get jobs in any defense plant.

Long adept at handling small amounts of money, she had

earned for several summers selling vegetables, Flora quickly saw this class as a means to earn money for college. Since she did not like the woman, she failed to discuss her plans with the teacher she was leaving. And this lady, who dated back to Carol and Jean's time, had become rather a prima donna, exerting much influence over who got any honor. She probably was miffed by Flora's oversight.

It wasn't that important to Flora, who already was looking forward to new adventures, and she was embarrassed that her mother made such a fuss about it. Daisy vented all her bitterness about the unfair treatment, even linking it to the predominant Catholic influence, to Juanita who listened patiently when she came to visit, and also to her husband.

Herb, long used to relieving his feelings by recounting his problems to Flora as they worked outside together, now restated all this to his daughter as if she were not even involved.

As often happens to the youngest child who is home alone with older parents, Flora listened to extended discussion about how her dad perceived his wife's mental condition which had not disappeared with the surgery. Once he described how he had taken Daisy to town for something and he felt she was dressed haphazardly, so before they left he urged her to fix her hair and put on a hat. The idea of a hat seemed to him to indicate more stability, Flora gathered, from his long, detailed account.

She somehow felt that the incident really indicated her mother's depressed mental condition, not contrariness as Herb seemed to think, but unable to articulate her thoughts on a subject she knew nothing about, she listened silently. Like all talkers, Herb felt better having told her about it.

That fall the Nortons received another jolt from an offspring. They had taken Neil's marriage to an uneducated,

Italian, former Catholic girl in stride but this news was harder to accept. Jean and Steve had left the Methodist church and become Mormons.

Herb and Daisy knew nothing about this religion; they had scarcely heard of it except in some uncomplimentary comments in Zane Grey's books of Western life. They finally learned that the Rankins had met with an immoral pastor in their own denomination which had propelled Steve to explore several religions, including Seventh Day Adventists. After long study and thought, he had decided to convert to the LDS faith, as the Church of Jesus Christ of Latter Day Saints was widely known.

Jean wrote glowing letters about how happy they were, leaving her parents dumbfounded. But since they were far away in Idaho, the only practical effect was that Herb now quit listening to the Tabernacle Choir program broadcast Sunday mornings from the LDS Temple in Salt Lake City. He had often enjoyed them now that he no longer attended church himself. Flora thought this rather funny.

Almost forgotten in the upset over their daughter's radical change in religion was the news that the Rankins had a second daughter in December 1942.

That Christmas was dull on the farm. Neil was in the service and could not return; Juanita was with her husband until he was shipped overseas; and Carol and John decided with gas rationing, that for once, they would spend the holiday with John's parents who lived much closer. Daisy knew she couldn't complain as Carol had faithfully spent nearly every Christmas since her marriage with them except the year her second child had been born in mid-December.

Daisy had relapsed from her months of high energy earlier in the year and with no one coming, she had neither heart nor strength to put up the usual decorations. Flora and her dad picked out what they considered a fine tree, as they had done for years, but the candles somehow did not shine as brightly as Flora remembered them in the years when there was more family, and thus some excitement.

She thought of the year Juanita had got her a pair of ice skates which she so much wanted, and the time when she was small that Floyd had been home for the holiday. That morning at breakfast everyone had found a shiny silver dollar at their plates. He had brought them back from Yellowstone Park where he had worked several summers earning college money. This year Flora spent much of Christmas Day reading The Forsythe Saga, putting it down only to help with the evening chores.

While Juanita was very proud of her husband, now a captain in the Air Force, and wrote glowing letters filled with patriotic fervor, her brother's letters to his parents were critical of the military. Daisy thought it a blessing he was not overseas where his letters would be censored. Worried over his wife, who was now pregnant, Neil's attitude was bad to start with, Daisy realized, although she couldn't help but agree with some of his caustic comments on how peppy band music was used to stir up patriotism. He was now at Yale University, teaching radio technology to young recruits.

Having to stand all day while he taught, he developed foot problems and soon he was found to have flat feet. What his family's concern was unable to do, this physical defect he probably had long had, won him an honorable discharge.

As Flora's high school graduation neared, Daisy began to hope they would soon be able to leave the farm. She had always felt this event was the milestone they needed to redirect their lives.

But she felt a more immediate need: Flora should have

some new clothes, at least a new graduation dress. Since she did not feel able to even go shopping with Flora, let alone make her new clothes as she had done for years, she again relied on Juanita, who was now back in Minneapolis while Leo was overseas. She had resumed work at the telephone company since, with the war, married women could continue to work.

Juanita obligingly brought several dresses up to the farm on approval one weekend and so Daisy had the satisfaction of her only daughter having a new graduation dress. It meant more to her than to Flora, who had had many nice homemade dresses over the years. She was not in any social whirl and knew she'd be leaving soon for work at Northwest Airlines in St. Paul, where most of her class had been hired, so she felt no need of new clothes.

Throughout her school years whenever there was a program or concert her mother had always made her a new dress. Daisy's procedure was to let the housework go and by the time the dress was hemmed-always late the night before the event-she would be exhausted. Flora came to feel it was not worth the stress to have a new dress.

The week after graduation she left for St. Paul, riding down with Mr. Ickler, and staying first with Juanita until she found housing. Daisy had hated to see her take the sheet metal course, knowing she would be mingling with mostly non-college bound girls. She fiercely wanted something better for her daughter than such a crowd.

Life seemed strangely quiet and empty for Herb and Daisy that summer, though their daughter wrote regularly and came home several weekends. Strawberries they had set out several years earlier were in their prime that year and Herb had to hire the Bissette girls to help him pick the abundant crop.

❀ Daisies Don't Tell

He agreed with Daisy there was no use to continue farming now with all the six children gone. He knew, despite her optimism that her health would improve, Daisy would need more medical care and it would be easier if they were in the Cities.

By August, the farm was sold to a physician in Croquille, who eventually built a modern home atop the hill to the west of the farmhouse along the sheep pasture. They would of course have electricity, Daisy thought bitterly.

She was so relieved about the sale that for once, she had scarce concern for the shock the loss of her childhood home had upon her daughter. Juanita also became sentimental and returned for a long weekend. Daisy was relieved when Flora quit her defense job and was safely enrolled at Graylin, where she had received a small scholarship.

The last weeks at the farm passed as if in a dream for Daisy. She worked frantically, throwing out many old items which could have become valuable later, such as the ornate pitcher and washbowl, left from the now discredited but once indispensable bedroom accessories. However, despite the years of hardship and sorrow, and knowing how much the place meant to at least the two youngest girls, Daisy took snapshots around the buildings and a final one of "her" three elms, now shading Ichler's house.

While she worked, or lay awake at night, her mind raced back to when she had first come to this farm twenty-four years ago. She had been idealistic, vigorous, and full of silent hope that she could raise Myrtie's children as a family and develop a lasting relationship with her brother-in-law. There had been many rough times, both financially and psychologically, with her nieces and nephews, but the rudder which had held her steady had been the knowledge of Herb's steadfast love. She thought fondly of how, despite his weariness, during the worst drought years he would carry pails of water from the stock tank to her sweet peas the last thing at night. He had managed to keep them blooming when all else was brown and bleached.

But there were many sacrifices on her part, too, like how she used the payments from loans she had made to several younger teachers she had helped in her own teaching days. Once during a particularly hard financial year, she had thankfully used the money for Christmas gifts for the children. She had cheerfully made many obvious sacrifices but honesty compelled her to admit many times of anger and unpleasantness. She shuddered to recall the time when Carol, who always argued with her the most vehemently, had caused Daisy to lose control and give the girl a frantic push. That would have ended it, but unfortunately the shove took place in the short hallway between kitchen and sitting room and Carol fell against the cellar door, knocking it open. Jean had cried out in horror as she saw her older sister falling down the stairs. But they were not steep and Carol was agile, catching her balance without coming to any harm.

On her final night in the big upstairs bedroom where much of the drama of her last quarter century had been played out, Daisy mused that of all the children, Carol and Neil had fought her the most. But, ironically, they were the ones who seemed the most attentive to their parents now.

But there were also funny recollections, despite the endless work, heat, and poverty. One time apples from the few remaining trees of a once flourishing orchard on the hillside west of the house had disappeared after being stored in the cellar. Daisy had first accused the children of taking them, but when it developed that no one had ever eaten one after they had been put in the basement, they knew something else had happened to them.

The next spring, when the last logs in the woodpile were moved, the lost apples were found, carefully cached away by squirrels. The furry thieves had long escaped justice.

As they drove down the winding country road for the last time, Herb slowed the car and looked back.

It's been a good farm, he thought. Twenty-five years of his life had been given to coaxing crops from the soil. He took satisfaction in the fact that despite their poverty, all his children now would have some education beyond high school and Myrtice's five were all self-sufficient.

He looked at Daisy beside him, noting how pale and weary she looked. "It's been a hard row, but we made it," he said, tenderly touching her hand.

She nodded silently, already looking forward eagerly to their new life. They were going to the Twin Cities where things would be better. As "her" three elms faded from view—but never from memory—Daisy thought, "I've done the best I could."